GREMMIE'S REEF

REAWAKENED WORLDS: VOLUME ONE

INTRODUCED BY LAURIE WINSLOW SARGENT

JOHN HAYDEN HOWARD

WildBluePress.com

GREMMIE'S REEF
REAWAKENED WORLDS VOLUME ONE published by:

WILDBLUE PRESS
P.O. Box 102440
Denver, Colorado 80250

ISBN 978-1-964730-40-0 Trade Paperback
ISBN 978-1-964730-41-7 eBook
ISBN 978-1-964730-42-4 Hardback

Cover design © 2023 WildBlue Press. All rights reserved.
Interior Formatting and Cover Design by Elijah Toten
www.totencreative.com

GREMMIE'S REEF

*This book is dedicated to the author's step-grandchildren,
Tyler, Aimee, Elisa, Jared, Eli, and Marissa, all whom
he dearly loved, and to his beloved wife, Jill.*

ACKNOWLEDGEMENTS

M any thanks from Laurie to her NC Writers critique group (AKA, cheerleaders.) Thanks also to Belinda Klau for her editorial wisdom and enthusiasm for this book, to agent Chip MacGregor of MacGregor & Luedeke Literary, and for the enduring fans of Hayden Howard.

CONTENTS

FOREWORD

by
Laurie Winslow Sargent

I knew John Hayden Howard affectionately as "Jack" for twenty-five years.

Born and raised in Santa Barbara, California, he was a confirmed bachelor (or so he thought) until age sixty-four. Then Jack met Jill.

I recall the day he and I (Jill's daughter) first met in 1989, three years after my father died. I was thirty-two years old at the time and a young mother. I had flown from Washington State to visit Mom. When I knocked on her door, it swung open to a tall, lanky man with longish gray hair covering his ears. He grinned broadly, stuck out his hand dramatically, and announced: "Hi! I'm Jack, and I'm in love with your mother!"

I smiled back awkwardly. Did she love him too? She did. They had met on a boat trip to the Catalina Islands. He was delighted to find a woman who'd boogie-board with him. She, a gutsy woman who frequently traveled to remote South American villages as a folk arts importer, was intrigued by his creativity and enjoyed his sense of humor.

As I got to know Jack, I learned that back in the 1950s–1960s he had written science fiction, including a novel. Yet only recently did I discover what a prolific and well-known author he was. It's been astonishing to learn he still has fans seventy years since his first stories were published. Most of his stories were published previously under his pen name Hayden Howard.

The author had 37 stories published in magazines 73 times, including in the US, UK, and Australia, with translations in Italian and French. Those stories included sci-fi short stories, sea stories, detective stories, and 1940s–1950s era fiction.

In Hayden's heyday—the fifties through the seventies—his stories were published in magazines, including *IF Worlds of Science Fiction*, *Planet Stories*, *Galaxy Science Fiction*, *Analog Science Fiction and Fact*, *Tales of the Sea*, and *Ellery Queen Mystery Magazine*. He also had two science fiction stories reprinted in anthologies. His story "Oil-Mad Bug-Eyed Monsters" was published in *BEST SF: 1970*, edited by Harry Harrison and Brian W. Aldiss (G.P. Putnam's Sons New York, 1971.) Another story, "To Grab Power," was reprinted in the paperback *Isaac Asimov's Wonderful Worlds of Science Fiction: 7 Space Shuttles* (edited by Isaac Asimov, Martin H. Greenberg, and Charles G. Waugh, published by New American Library, NAL Penguin Inc, 1987.)

Most of Hayden's stories are Earth-bound with futuristic tech; others take place in spaceships or on other planets. His main characters vary from students, to scientists, to surfers, to professors and time-travelers. In this volume, expect every story to take you to an entirely different time and place. Most of Hayden's stories have surprise endings—much like the old television show *The Twilight Zone,* the 1959-1964 science fiction horror anthology created and hosted by Rod Serling.

Ten years ago I should have realized that Jack, as Hayden, was well-known for his writing. When I was living in Iowa, a friend from Estonia—yes, the country—mentioned he loved sci-fi. When I mentioned the name Hayden Howard, he instantly recognized it. The man led me to his office to show me not only his vintage sci-fi collection but also Hayden Howard's biography in *The Encyclopedia of Science Fiction*. The online version of that encyclopedia lists many of Hayden's published science fiction stories, plus his Nebula and Hugo Award nominations.

Hayden was in good company. Other Nebula nominations in the 1960s included J.R.R. Tolkien's *Lord of the Rings* series. Hayden was prolifically published in magazines with authors Jack London, Frank Herbert (the author of *Dune*), Isaac Asimov, Philip K. Dick, Robert Silverberg, and other well-known sci-fi authors.

I'm mystified and chagrined now that I did not realize most of this until after he passed away. Yet during the decades I knew him, he was devoted to his beloved wife and to traveling with her. He was delighted to be Grandpa Jack to my three children as they grew from toddlerhood to adulthood. He was a cheerleader for me, in my own book and magazine article writing, and wrote clever poems for his grandchildren and wife, until passing in 2014, at age 88. In his later years, it seems that for him family trumped fame.

Meanwhile, during those decades Jack and Jill were married, his half-century-old manuscripts were hidden under massive paper piles in his upstairs back office. The door could barely be nudged open. And since he never boasted about his past successes, we had no idea what that office held other than old financial or family papers. To be honest, it was a paper tiger I never hoped to tangle with.

After Jack died, I helped Mom move closer to me. Jack's papers came with her, including all his original manuscripts. Then in 2017, after Mom also passed away, as executor I inherited the many boxes of Hayden's papers. I was reluctant to sneeze my way through them—whatever they held—expecting a tedious operation. So the boxes were hidden again, in my own attic, until a move of my own forced me to deal with those dratted papers.

I contacted SFWA (Science Fiction and Fantasy Writers of America) to see if any university might want

Hayden Howard's old manuscripts, in particular the typed manuscript for his novel. What gave me pause was that the sci-fi archives wanted them ALL. A contact there said they were eager and willing to pay all shipping costs for three large, heavy boxes of yellowed, unsorted papers. They said even his editing scribbles would be of interest. Hmm. I did send for archival the manuscript for his novel, yet kept Hayden's rights to the material. However, as I considered shipping the rest, I became more curious.

Finally motivated, I sorted through Jack's papers with a dust mask on. To my amazement, I found over forty stories (plus three to four versions of many). Wonderful stories with creative twists.

At that point, I still had no idea how many of his stories had been published, so I finally did an internet deep-dive on Jack's pen name, Hayden Howard, and found he also wrote under his full name, John Hayden Howard.

Seven of Hayden's sci-fi stories were in his Esk Series, published in *Galaxy Science Fiction* (April 1965-April 1967), later compiled into his novel: *The Eskimo Invasion* (New York: Ballantine Books.) That book, nominated for the 1967 Nebula Award: Best Novel, was about an alien invasion transforming a group of indigenous people into an apparently benign, fast-breeding new species, called Esks.

Hayden's original novelette in that series, included in this book, was nominated for the 1966 Nebula Award: Best Novelette, and the 1967 Hugo Award for Best Novelette. I renamed that story "Arctic Invasion" as the term "Eskimo" has less wide use now for describing the Inuit people than in previous years, yet retained that term in the story since that was the only proper term in the 1960s. Also bear in mind that the alien people portrayed in the story were mysteriously unlike them.

It's a treat for me to compile Hayden's 1950s-'60s published works, but also stories not previously published and hidden until now. Consider yourselves his first readers for stories written 60-70 years ago. How exciting is that?

The first story in this collection, "The Tragedy of Henry Diddoh," was written in 1951, when Hayden was about 26 years old. In that story, his character Henry finds a way to be two places at the same time. While the end results are bound to be disastrous, the surprise ending with his counterpart, Hank, is distressing yet fitting.

Hayden's stories offer an intriguing window into the 1950s and 60s, with "the future" apparently (in his mind then) being the 1990s. Remarkably, in the '50s he wove into his stories technology we use regularly in the twenty-first century but only dreamt of back then. In a story I'm using in a future volume, one character uses a "visaphone" to videochat in a way we now use Skype or Zoom software.

Hayden's old manuscripts, though in perfect manuscript format, were typed by him on a typewriter on musty now-yellowed paper. That did not lend well to scanning, so to digitize Hayden's stories I spoke them into my own "visaphone"—my iPhone, which I also use now to Skype and Facetime with Hayden's own great-grandchildren. The 1950s Jack would have gotten a big kick out of knowing that, had he been able to peek into the real future.

Or was Hayden a time traveler, himself?

PART 1: WHAT IF

THE TRAGEDY OF HENRY DIDDOH

Written in St. Augustine, Florida in 1951
Setting: A University Town with a Secret Laboratory

Henry

If not for a bizarre and unexpected opportunity, Associate Professor of American Literature Henry Diddoh might have endlessly drifted overcoated over hilly sidewalks to lectures and recitation, cups of coffee, and sly hands of three no-trump with smiling, smoke-veiled diners replete with witty forays against the board. At each day's end, ducking against the wind, he would head home to students' hopeless bluebooks and a bottle of 1812 Cabernet glinting evilly in the cabinet.

He may have drifted thusly, generations of bay-chilled wind imperceptibly wearing him to his soul. . . until he smiled up from his coffin, shabby-suited and content.

But he was not a robot, he was a man.

One weekday morning, Mrs. Parr—who occupied the fifth floor of the apartment tower and whose ceiling clung to Henry's sixth floor residence—did not awake on schedule. For the punctual shuffle of Henry's feet, as he usually dressed for his *From Poe to Faulkner* class, missed a day. The rhythm was broken.

Henry Diddoh was then 36 years old. He looked younger, felt older, except on Sundays when he visited his high blood-pressured mother and became quite a hopeless young man again, nervous-eyed in the labyrinth of her advice. "You should get married," she'd say. "No, better yet, you should write a book."

To him, the latter advice seemed preferable, although typewriters behaved schizophrenically beneath his fingers. Marriage, he intimated, meant fettering a free soul. A wife, dearly beloved though she might be, would (now, get this!) channel him into a routine.

His routine was rarely sour.

Yet at times, for example at the salaciously bare university Junior-Senior Hijinks, he remembered how lonely he was, though lonely was not quite the word. He would smile, blink his eyes and peer about. He had a beautiful smile, the kind that made sorority pledges feel like little mothers who could take him by the ears and kiss him soundly. But to faculty, even with most honorable intentions, coeds were taboo. And his academic position was his life.

So Henry mastered the harmless great-uncle façade. Wistfully he wanted to eat his marital cake and have his free soul too, without seriously tempting himself to an extramarital slice. For he held himself a pure white torch of whatever universities stand for—and also problems might ensue.

The lucky recipient of all this white heat, if she did not choose to blackmail him, might drag him to the altar (for he feared he was a soft-hearted fellow.) Worse yet, he'd be found out and summarily excommunicated by the jealous faculty.

So he drifted safe in indecision. In fifteen or twenty years, by the time he was Dean, any decision would be safe and academic.

Without warning, one day, a pair of shiny lips, and uplifted set of mammae—spiritedly aimed at him—shattered his routine, his future. That was enough. Henry was breast to breast with indecision. Unfortunately, as he had always feared, she was an undergrad. She was a smooth-skinned brunette in his *Contemporary American Lit* course. While he discoursed on the terse dialogues of Hemingway, he could feel the pleading heat of her large, brown eyes. She had a fine mind too, he told himself.

He did not intend to take advantage of this earnestly offered felicity. He must either send her away crying— the wisest choice— or carry on with bated breath until the end of the semester, when they might send engraved announcements to the world and hope for faculty mercy. For American lit profs were ten cents a bunch, and he had not made as many faculty friends as he should have. And regarding breaking unwritten laws, the Administration would not mail a We Regret slip— there were subtler means.

Either of the two choices would cause pain.

Fortunately, or perhaps unfortunately, as the result of a long, off-the-record talk with Professor Renworth of the Physiology Department concerning an unusual experiment, Henry's choices increased to three.

Henry Diddoh paid his fated visit to the lab where Renworth, a dabbler in neural electronics, was probing a handsome cadaver. The body's lifelike twitching made Henry's Adam's apple return distress signals.

The muscular young man on the slab, Renworth explained, had received a 38-caliber bullet through his cerebellum while jimmying the cash register of an all-night filling station. The man had survived in a coma long enough for Renworth to extralegally acquire him, then chemically hibernate his life processes.

Now the once-a-cadaver's heart pumped again under its own power. The thalamic portion of his brain seemed in excellent condition. His blue-framed pupils dilated as efficiently as ever when Renworth shaded them with his hand.

A finger drawn across the bottom of his foot made his big toe curl downward in the Babinski reflex of a complete idiot. Renworth explained that an electro scalpel had removed any memories or brain matter that could store new experiences above the purely reflexive level.

Henry stared at the twitching young man with fascinated disgust.

"Now Henry, please don't laugh or take offense, but I've been studying you for several semesters."

Henry's jaw dropped.

"I have a favor to ask," Renworth continued. "My attention has been attracted by your extraordinarily developed capacity to engage in several intellectual processes at one time. They say Julius Caesar could do nine—or was it seven—things at once. I've watched you in the faculty lounge, simultaneously playing out a bridge contract and carrying on multiple relatively intelligent conversations, while also rechecking students' bluebooks and waggling your foot in time to the radio.

"Once, when you rose to meet your one o'clock class, the lecture cards that were blank when you had dealt out the first hand were miraculously darkened with notes. Yet from what I hear, your lectures, while nowise deep, are sufficiently well prepared."

Renworth leaned across the body. "And through it all, in the lounge, you smile and laugh without strain— as though such multiple efforts are second nature to you." His smile was flattering. But…

Henry's boyish face showed pain, for he considered his lectures invariably deep.

"Now, Henry, we've always been close friends and I'm in a position to speak up for you," said Renworth, alluding to intricate political maneuvers necessary to advancement in academic ranks.

"I've fitted this young, superbly healthy, organism with one station of the neural broadcasting apparatus Planesein left in his laboratory. Planesein's notes were fragmentary; I think his suicide was an impulse because he was normally a most systematic man.

"Apparently his results were disappointing, because his subjects—having minds of their own—subconsciously resisted his invasion of their bodily controls."

Renworth unwrapped a cluster of wires and batteries suggesting a complex hearing aid.

"Of course, he got very nice images through their eyes—heard his own voice pleading with them to cooperate, felt the itch beneath one grad student's girdle. But when he thought for her to spit on the floor, she managed to restrain herself. After he disconnected her, she said she was confused as to whether the thoughts were hers or his.

"Planesein was also troubled by increasingly severe headaches and a lost feeling as though he were in a waking dream. I've had similar symptoms. I'm not sure at all times whether I'm in this fellow or in myself. Splitting one's perception into two compartments, doubling one's brainwork, is for a rather average man like myself a terrific strain.

"It's infinitely more difficult, for example, than what Mormunski does every Saturday on the football field: fading back, avoiding charging linemen while simultaneously watching a receiver streaking down a sideline. A good passer needs the ability to split his vision; the man to operate this fellow must have much rarer ability."

Revulsion and curiosity wavered on Henry's face. From bridge-table conversations, he knew some of the electronic factors involved. The subject's brainwaves initiated by basic stimuli—sight, sound, and tactile sense—were literally broadcast to the operator's equipment, modified by his own psychosomatic system, then rebroadcast to the subject in a continuous stream of communication. All with the speed of stimulus response within a single individual. One brain struggled to translate two sets of sensory impressions into two sets of motor responses.

No wonder Renworth had looked seedy lately, as their bridge partners had said. The consensus of those unqualified to know was that the experiments were a complete failure. A man can hardly think for himself. How can he do that for two? Especially when the subject can't help but resist. But they did not know about the young man on the slab.

"Let me try it on for just a moment."

The first thing Henry said after that was: "I'm cold; put some clothes on the poor devil."

"No, make him say it."

After some brow-furrowing on Henry's part, the cadaver sat up, and managed in a voice curiously like Henry's—although it should have seemed deeper—"I'm cold. Put some clothes on the poor devil."

Henry turned angrily to Renworth, for already he was beginning to identify with the subject. The cadaver's voice rushed: "When did you feed me last? I have a pain in my stomach and my head hurts. The connection behind my ears is too tight."

Henry lifted off his own connection. "This is interesting—exciting, I must say. But let's warm this fellow up and feed him before I continue. I see no purpose in my suffering his pains."

"He can't eat without your thought patterns."

"Feed him intravenously," Henry suggested.

"That won't ease his stomach spasms. If you cooperate, we'll have him feeling better than you ever have." Renworth continued enthusiastically. "He's a big healthy young man, who will fill you with the flush joy of life, with the pride of his body. Presumably, if you can handle him, you'll be in a position to enjoy many things you may have been too timid or anemic to do. Practice with him until the end of the semester. Then, if you've achieved fair motor control, we'll open a few eyes at the national convention!"

"One thing," Renworth added. "I've put a lot of time and equipment into this fellow. Don't stray too far from your normal caution. Dissipation, a fall, a fight, syphilis, or malnutrition could spoil him—would spoil him more easily than a man."

"Really," snapped Henry. "What kind of man do you think I am?" He redonned the equipment; the part above his shirt collar could easily pass for a hearing aid.

In spite of his physical discomfort, the muscular young man smiled. "You can call me Hank."

Henry and Hank grinned at each other like a pair of newly successful ventriloquists.

At first, Henry came to the lab to practice. Soon, however—as a photographer who learns to erect the inverted ground glass image in his mind—Henry found he could send Hank wandering over sidewalks, shut out from the consciousness that was checking bluebooks. He could operate Hank and make him pass quite plausibly as a human being, without thinking about it at all.

When he, or rather, Hank, told Renworth this, the physiologist was astounded.

"You're even more talented than I hoped, Henry. After we've unveiled my success, so to speak, we can start looking for practical applications. Keep it up! By summer, at the rate you're improving, no one will know this cadaver from a conscious, even intelligent man."

Hank, part-time-Henry, smiled.

Hank

The professor had underestimated him. He was a man *now*. And as Hank walked the streets, he worried about summer, when the experiment with him might end.

Soon Hank found he did not have to sleep just because Henry dozed off. Yet he did learn that when he took a bus out of the city, he had to pull the stop cord at about 20 miles from Henry. If he traveled much farther, his sight blurred.

While Henry lectured, Hank listened and was disappointed. But he did not reveal this to Henry verbally, the only way he could communicate with him now. A wall had sprung up between their thoughts.

Henry had told Hank he was a busy man. He was worrying about what he should do about his girlfriend Julia, so was glad not to have to bother with Hank. Renworth was busy too, preparing midterm questions. He treated Hank as if he were an idiot and did not urge him to stay at the lab.

Hank saw with chagrin how Henry and Julia held hands in little cafés where they were not apt to be seen by Henry's colleagues. Hank stalked the lonely streets. He was grateful for the food, bed, and pocket money Henry gave him. But he became angry when he thought of Henry and Julia, for he was part Henry too. Their memories were a common pool; the way he talked, his mannerisms, and the way he saw the world was Henry's. He was equally the man who thrilled at Julia's touch. Yet he was shut out.

As Henry's "nephew," Hank should have been introduced to Julia, but wasn't. The people he did meet—after initial friendliness—seemed to lose interest. Some made vaguely sarcastic remarks, as if he irritated them. He overheard one Tri-Delt say he talked like a stuffy old professor, then speculate that maybe it was an egotistical phase he was going through.

So Hank decided to change. He saw himself reflected in the eyes and the actions of students seen around the campus, people in stores, waitresses, newsboys: he was a good looking, apparently easygoing fellow in his early twenties. Gradually his personality merged with the superficial reflection. Less and less in his thoughts was he an over-punctual scholar named Henry Diddoh.

One day, Hank watched some undergrads playing touch football at North Field. One of them twisted their knee.

When they invited him to fill in at the end, he hesitated, for his alter ego Henry had never been much for athletics. But Hank's quick reflexes and strong body made up for Henry's lack of experience.

In the joy of running, blocking, feeling his muscles, being slapped on the back as one of the boys, he felt the thrill and pride Henry had never experienced. Hank knew he was not that musty, inhibited little man.

Determined to complete himself, to become a wholly separate man, he announced to Henry he was going to get a job with room and board as a hasher at a fraternity house. He wanted to be on his own. He didn't want to accept Harry's money anymore, so even a lowly dishwashing job would do.

As Hank stood with Henry before the tall floor-to-ceiling window in Henry's apartment, with the lights of the city at his back, Henry smiled. Hank smiled too, seeing the humor of it: Henry as Hank, locked inside the same skull with Henry, was saying goodbye to Henry.

Henry said, "I wish you luck. I won't stand in your way. I'll talk to Renworth after midterm. It will be bad if he's planning for any reason to disconnect you in order to use you in further experiments."

Hank winced.

Henry nodded rather sadly. "You may not have time, or you may want to use your time in purely physical realization. But with your brain, it seems a pity you don't begin the novel I've always been too busy to write."

They shook hands, and Henry promised never to disconnect, nor leave the city without taking Hank along, and to stall Renworth if he wanted to do further experiments before summer. "Yet," he cautioned Hank, "I wouldn't plan my life beyond summer and the National Convention of Physiologists, if I were you."

In the basement of the frat house, Hank had the shadow of death, less than two months away now, and loneliness for

Julia to keep him awake. He decided he'd better have a talk with Renworth himself. For the professor to turn him off would be the same as murder.

He was frightened when he knocked on the door of Renworth's back-of-the-lot cottage.

When Renworth led him into the lamplight, he seemed happy enough to see him, although his eyes kept wandering to a huge pile of midterm bluebooks on the table of his cramped living-dining room. He looked at Hank. "How are you managing this fellow, Henry?"

"Please, doctor, you aren't talking to Henry anymore. I've become a separate personality."

"Merely an illusion, Henry. I had no idea the experiment would go to this extreme. If we aren't careful, this might leave you with permanent duality—schizoid, confused."

"No!" Hank leaned heavily across the table, upsetting the pile of bluebooks. "I am *not* Henry."

"You have a remarkable brain capacity to achieve such a convincing split," Renworth's voice soothed. "But you'll be more content when you are unified again."

With a deceptive step toward a bluebook that had slithered to the floor, Renworth snatched at Hank's connection. But Hank was too quick for him. They grappled. Hank hooked his leg behind the physiologist's, and he shoved the man to the floor. He knew Renworth would make sure he was disconnected now. Renworth would claim he was a violent maniac.

As the physiologist rose, breathing hard, Hank snatched an Indian blanket from the wall. Whirling, he cupped the man in it before he could reach the door. They fell, Renworth shouting dimly through the blanket, but Hank was much stronger. He was quite truly acting in self-defense as he pressed folds of wool against the man's twisting face. For Renworth to disconnect Hank would be to kill him, and Renworth would do that. Hank pressed until the man's gasps faded away.

Frantically Hank looked about, trying to remember things Henry had read, detective movies he'd seen. He could hardly make it look like an accident and report it himself. He had no draft card, no identification papers, no history. No history, that is, until they checked his fingerprints and found they matched those of a supposedly-dead filling station bandit.

He could not flee the city because his brain was in Henry. But he dared not tell Henry. Henry would simply tell the authorities the truth. No, Henry would be in a spot himself; the law would not understand this mess at all.

But Henry might tell. About the time the newspapers got a hold of it, Henry would commit suicide, execute them both; he was not the type to bear up under that sort of thing. And he would feel guilty. He would not try to escape bodily from the city. He would simply put a bullet through their heads.

Yet Henry was innocent. Hank reviled himself: Henry never thought to hurt anyone in his life.

Gradually Hank began to see order in the cluttered room and the body he knelt across. His only course, for Henry's sake as well as his own, was to commit a "perfect crime." Apart from Henry, no one would suspect the motive. It was likely no one knew he had come to the cottage tonight. That was in their favor too.

Quickly he unwrapped the man and began artificial respiration. He remembered the gist of something Henry had read: proud police records and crime-does-not-pay movies to the contrary, the number of known murders each year was well in excess of the number of apprehensions. And the number of murders unrecognized as such probably surpassed either figure.

Carefully he dragged the gently breathing man into the kitchenette. Folding his hand about Renworth's, he opened the oven door, then turned the gas handle.

Wrinkling his nose at the smell of it, he eased the psychologist's head and shoulders inside—careful not to skin his face—and waited a long time after the man had stopped breathing. He stared at the pilot light; that was shielded against explosion. He turned one of the burners low, using the man's hand again, and lit it.

Then he dragged Renworth back into the living room, arranged his clothing and slumped him at the table. The skinned place on his cheek due to abrasion from the stiff wool blanket could not be disguised. Probably the skin about his ribs was red and from the artificial respiration.

He realized there was saliva on the blanket. Back into the stinking kitchen he went, dampened a rag, then hurried out. Leaving the kitchen door open and the gas still on, he wiped off and rehung the blanket.

Blinking, he went into the kitchen again, closed one open window, and found a dust cloth. He wiped the table, doorknob, and edge of the door. Then while shielding his hand with the cloth, he pushed in the lower button at the door so it would lock when he closed it from outside. He returned the cloth through the gas-flooding rooms, glanced at the open flame, then used his handkerchief to open the door.

He walked slowly down the path beneath the questioning stars, then along the sidewalk to the frat house. When he reached home, in case his clothing carried a slight odor of gas, he changed, then joined two pledges rolling dice against the baseboard and chatted with them. He returned to his basement cell. . . and no sleep.

L ater there was a dull thump, then the wail of fire engines.

One of the pre-med students read the morning paper aloud with glee; he knew he had screwed up his physiology midterm. "It says, 'The heroism of our fire department rescued many of Dr. Renworth's furnishings.' Nothing about the bluebooks though; you'd think they would've burned. 'Dr. Renworth's body was hurled across the table by the force of the initial blast. His face was seared before Hoseman Adamic could remove him.' If it seared his face, it should've seared my bluebook."

Hank felt horrified at the student's nonchalance.

After breakfast, Hank went to the lab. He had to wait till noon to enter though, before some prying graduate students left. He raised a newspaper before his face as they passed because he had never been sure how Renworth had kept the secret of the alive cadaver. One of the students may have peeked in. It would be quite a sensation if Hank were recognized and would surely lead to a police investigation.

Extracting all recent notes concerning the neural electronic experiment from Renworth's filing cabinet, Hank folded them inside the newspaper. If inquisitive people missed them, they'd probably blame the disappearance on earlier snoopers.

After he burned the notes, he drove to put the whole mess from his mind. It helped that the coroner listed the death as accidental. The conclusion was that Dr. Renworth had lit one of the stovetop burners, turned it very low, then turned on the oven but forgot to light that, and had fallen asleep without noticing the smell of escaping gas.

The day Hank finally went to Henry, he found him sitting by his high front window looking more nervous than usual. From the neat dark blue suit he wore, it was apparent he was just back from the funeral.

"I suppose you read about Dr. Renworth, Hank."

Hank nodded somberly. He was not acting.

"Hank, I don't know what to say to you. I can hardly press you to appear before that physiologists' meeting. I don't think Renworth ever told anyone about you. A few of his students may have seen you on the slab, but you look quite different. More a cultured man now."

Henry stared out the window, down at the sidewalk six stories below. "Of course, I'm really talking to myself. Perhaps I'm insane, or you're really a man with a brain of your own and it was all a confusing joke of Renworth's."

Hank found a laugh in his throat. "I feel quite real. My origin may be odd, but as Descartes put it: 'I think, therefore I am.' You know I'm part of you; and I'm also myself. I want to live my own life, win recognition, have people like me, find love, just as you do. Just because my consciousness and body are connected only by radio waves doesn't mean I'm any less a man. Henry, you won't tell anybody about me, will you?"

"Of course not. How are you coming with the novel?"

"Would you like to read the synopsis? I'll bring it over tomorrow night."

"Hank, could I take a rain check on that? I have a dinner date with Julia."

"Did you ever ask her to marry you?"

"No, my mother hasn't been well lately," said Henry. "Say, would you like to see Mother? I could say you're a prize student."

"Thank you, I'd rather not. I never think about her, and it might be disturbing."

The next night, as Hank scraped endless piles of fraternity dishes, no less greasy for their fancy coat-of-arms, he thought about Henry and Julia eating together, holding hands, kissing. A dish slipped through his fingers and shattered in the sink.

"Hey Hanky-panky, those cost money."

"Okay, okay, okay!"

"Well, don't get hard-nosed. We aren't asking you to pay for it, are we?"

Why didn't Henry be a man and marry her? Why did he keep stringing her along? All that guff about his mother. Henry had a spine like a pipe cleaner. He was nearly twice her age. He was an old maid with trousers. He wouldn't be real enough for a lovely young thing like Julia.

She should marry someone near her own age, Hank thought. Hank, in fact.

He knew, with his physique and knowledgeable air, he could have almost any girl on campus that could be had. But he held back because he was in love with Julia, although there was something pretty rotten about horning in on Henry.

Henry couldn't help the way things were. This was probably Henry's last chance. If he didn't find someone, when his mother died, he might go to pieces.

So Hank and Julia had never met. Until…

"Oh, wait, aren't you Henry's nephew?"

"How do you know that?"

"One noon hour I saw you when Henry and I drove past the apartment. You were sitting on the front lawn, reading. Henry didn't stop though. He's unfriendly sometimes. Things worry him—the Board, some of those snippy-nosed profs, that tragedy of Dr. Renworth. The first thing he said was: 'he killed him.' Oh, I'm sorry. I don't know why I rushed all that at you, when I've never met you before."

"Well, he *is* my uncle." Hank smiled down at her rosy face. It had been a long time since Henry had looked at her like that. Hank would look at her like that all the time.

"He said you're writing a novel." She smoothed down her skirt. "He seems very proud of you."

"I'm struggling with writing one."

Unconscious of pedestrians flowing about them, they talked for a long time. She said she could tell he and Henry were related. They smiled and talked alike, although Henry used more two-bit words. They didn't *look* at all alike, but that didn't make any difference to her. She said she could see right through that.

"I've been so curious to meet you, Hank. Henry always thinks of an excuse not to introduce us. Are you the family's black sheep?" She had a gorgeous smile.

He grinned and nodded.

"So that's it. I'll bet I never would've met you if I hadn't waylaid you just now."

Hank asked, "What makes you say that? Surely, you would see me at the wedding."

She scuffed the pavement with the outer edge of her white oxford. "Henry is taking an awful lot for granted telling you that. He hasn't even asked me. When I wrote to mother about him, she wasn't at all pleased. I *am* awfully young for him. Not that that matters.

"It's just that sometimes he's so deep. I don't know whether he's going to kiss me or shake my hand and say, 'bye, bye, little girl.' And I assure you I am not, definitely not, a little girl."

"Come on," said Hank sadly. "I'll buy you a Coke."

That night, he broke another dish.

When he took the automatic elevator to Henry's apartment, there was perspiration on his hands. Rather briskly, because he was embarrassed and unhappy about it, he told Henry he was in love, was still in love that is, with Julia.

After a pained silence Henry replied. "All right." He paused, then added, "You know I could disconnect you."

"Yes."

"I feel responsible for you, though. I began this mess."

Hank chuckled ruefully. "That feeling is mutual. It was just as much me that put on this damned apparatus for the first time."

"Hank, you know I'm not considering turning you off. If you want to try to take Julia, that's your decision. May the best man win, and all that sort of rot. And bad luck to you!" Henry managed to smile.

They shook hands like uncomfortable school boys, and Hank went away ashamed.

But two nights later, when her voice called after him, his feet stopped.

"Now I'll buy *you* a Coke." She led him into the bowling alley. No need for secrecy, as there had to be when she was with her professor.

In the nights that followed, they bowled and danced. They went to a great flaming football rally in the Bowl and threw their beer cans on the bonfire along with the other revelers.

Afterward, as they swung down the hill, Julia laughed. "You're a funny boy, Hank. You're all friendliness and personality during the evening. Then when you walk me home, you start pouting and frowning like an old man."

He turned savagely toward her, surprising even himself. "We've got to tell Henry, or I've got to stop seeing you. I can't...."

Her finger barred his lips. "I've already told him. I said I like him more than anyone I know, but that he's more like a father to me. You see, he finally asked me to marry him."

Hank pushed her hand away.

"Don't, Hank. Afterward, when I kissed him, he was about ready to cry, and I already was. But he's a wonderful man. He said, 'I suppose Hank is waiting for you.' I didn't know what to say to that, so I didn't say anything."

Hank found a full-time job in a book and art supply store. Near the end of the semester, they eloped one weekend to a plush hotel—in the city, of course. Julia had wanted to return to her hometown and family to be married, but naturally Hank had to talk her out of that and fudge a few facts on the marriage certificate. He could hardly ask

Henry to accompany them out of town. Seeing the swollen appearance of Henry's face from a distance, Hank realized he must be taking it very hard.

When Hank knocked on his door and called his name, he heard someone move about inside, but the door did not open. Hank went away feeling it might be for the best if they didn't see each other. Hank hated to be reminded that the body married to Julia was a near brainless idiot's. That gave him a guilty feeling he had never experienced, even from Renworth's death.

The second publisher to whom Hank sent his novel synopsis and sample chapters offered him a $500 advance and an invitation – or was it a command? – to fly to New York. But finals were in progress; Henry could hardly accompany him. Hank put it off and telegraphed excuses to the publisher. He could not bring himself to telephone Henry.

Henry finally telephoned Hank in July. They chatted as though they were friends. Henry explained he did not want to see Hank and Julia together because of the painful emotional twist it would give him. He said he had been in a depressed state the latter part of the semester but felt easier now. As usual, he wanted to take his mother to Sealow for the summer, unless it was imperative that Hank remain in the city.

Hank agreed to travel too and stay near Sealow, in Carmel. Beneath a cypress tree, Hank and Julia summered in a cheap trailer court. His advance on the novel had melted away and checks from his bookstore job ended. But they were happy. He spent long hours rewriting the novel. When they returned to the city, he found a job as copywriter for a weekly shopping newspaper.

He and Julia did not cross paths with Henry in Carmel, nor in the city.

Late in the fall semester, Hank's novel about the vicissitudes of a man trying to conceal a split personality was published after a meager advertising and distribution campaign. Reviewers thought it not too convincing, but driblets of royalties began in the nick of time. Julia was expecting a baby in the spring.

One evening, while Hank was typing an outline for his second novel, the keys blurred before his eyes. He rushed out to the used car he'd bought; Henry must be leaving the city.

As he turned the key in the ignition, his fingers, once he told them what to do, seemed deft enough. The dulling was in his brain rather than in his body, opposite of the sensation he'd had when he experimentally went near the end of communication range with Henry. Then the brain was clear. Now it was drunk.

Blearily crawling the car down back streets, he reached Henry's tower apartment building. When Hank got up to his door, his hammering fist swung it open. He made out Henry sitting on the floor. As Hank steered him toward the shower, Henry said brightly: "I killed him."

"Long time ago," Henry burbled and slurred, "I better take notes before they find out about me. Gone. All shummer I worry about this. Deducshun. I turned on the gas while he was asleep and took the notes to cover my filthy trail and did not want to be remembered of it." Henry looked lopsided.

Hank's words staggered across the gap to his tongue. "Henry, I . . . some graduate students took the notes, filthy fellows."

Chattering in the icy shower, Henry managed: "Never did it. Never."

After Hank returned home, he wearily assured Julia he'd left earlier because he thought he'd left a hotplate on in the newspaper office. He tried to conceal his splitting headache. At least he did not develop the stomach symptoms of a hangover.

In the morning, Henry telephoned to apologize; it would never happen again.

But two weeks later, his mother suffered her first stroke, paralyzing her left side. The second killed her.

At the funeral, when Hank looked down into her neatly arranged face, he felt no emotion at all. He tried to console Henry, even urged him to stay at his home for a while. The suddenly-old-faced professor glared at him speechlessly, as if the inevitable was his fault.

Two mornings later, Hank moaned and tossed, unable to wake up. His wife telephoned the doctor: delirium, she said. The doctor wore a puzzled expression when he left. By afternoon, Hank was able to go to the office. He did not call Henry this time; he knew how it was.

But the next afternoon, when he recovered from a second all-night drunk, Hank was frightened. If this continued, both would lose their jobs. Not only was the baby coming, he must meet payments on both home and automobile.

He went to see Henry. "Come live with us for a while; it will do you good to see Julia. When she has the baby, you'll feel it's yours too."

Henry stared solemnly at him from his befouled bed. "You're merely worried I'll spoil your happiness. You tricked Julia; you were afraid to tell her you're not a man. No, I'm sorry I said that. Just go away, so I won't have to look at you. And don't worry; I finished the bottle."

For a week Henry met his classes. But through the student grapevine, Hank heard that old man Diddoh was losing his marbles. He repeated himself so much, his lectures were more boring than usual. He gave all his students 'As' on their Walden essays.

Hank could only hope Henry would last the semester. Then a vacation might snap him out of it. Understandably, he did not seek psychiatric help for Henry.

When Hank turned to the second section of one morning paper, he saw in great black letters: LOCAL PROFESSOR

QUIZZED BY BOARD FOR CUFFING HONOR STUDENT. Henry Diddoh had repeated himself way too often. When a boy tittered, the professor stalked him from the rostrum and slapped him across the face.

The board suspended him with a warning.

At the newspaper, Hank had a dizzy spell and asked the office girl to drive him home.

He then made his way to Henry's apartment. Henry insisted he had been unable to face his classes and had needed to pour himself a stiff one.

Hank urged him to resign due to ill health, to find a new position when he felt better. Perhaps he would be happier working for a newspaper. Hank could get him a job. Or Henry could write a novel himself. Julia and Hank were short of cash, but they could get a loan on the car. That way Henry wouldn't have to worry about money while he worked on his novel. Hank knew Henry's tiny savings had been exhausted by his mother's illness and burial.

"No, I appreciate your offers, but I'm going to stick out the semester. I notified the Dean that I'll meet my Wednesday classes."

Wednesday, Hank rose, staggered to the bathroom, and fell heavily across the basin. As he crawled in beside Julia again, he prayed Henry was not trying to go to class in his condition.

When she woke, he told her he had a stomach upset. But soon he announced he felt better, then called a taxi. He was afraid to drive the car, and of course it would not do to have Julia drive him to Henry's apartment. That would only raise more questions in her mind. He had her worried enough as it was.

As he lunged into the cab, he noticed that although his brain seemed clearer, his muscular coordination was weakening. Henry must be leaving the city and already be over the 20-mile limit. Since the ocean was to the west, there were three directions left, so he told the cabbie to drive north as fast as he could. Hank occasionally saw his hand before his face. He then mumbled to the puzzled driver to turn around and speed south.

Communication between his brain and body were fading less rapidly now, but still fading. He knew Henry must be on the main highway. There was no hope of the cab getting through the city streets. When Hank passed out, the man would probably take him to a hospital.

Pushing clumsily at the cabbie's shoulder, he signed for him to stop. Hank thrust some bills at his querulous voice, staggered to the sidewalk, and waved for him to drive away. The blur of the cab faded as he crawled into a thick hedge. He felt resistance from it, but not its individual thorns.

Soon Hank was entirely disconnected from his body. His thoughts, undistracted by sensory perceptions, were frighteningly clear. If Henry did not turn back within a day or two, Hank's brainless body would die of starvation or exposure. Unless he were discovered—in which case his communication apparatus would be disconnected or damaged by curious doctors.

He should have taken out some life insurance. No, that would have required a medical exam…

Gradually, since his brain was not receiving any stimulating signals from Henry, against his will, Hank lost consciousness.

Fuzzy leaves appeared above his eyes, their outlines sharpening against the cloud-streamed sky. He heard an occasional fringe of footsteps, soft, then loud, then quiet again. When he finally sat up and brushed away the blanket of sodden leaves, he was shivering. He sneezed as he rose stiffly and staggered down the street. A boy at the corner stared at him, clutching a newspaper's bright comic section. It must be Saturday or Sunday.

Hank began to run.

His wife opened the door, red-eyed and swollen faced, her mother standing behind her. They had called the police, Julia said. Hank slumped on the sofa, his arm about her. He managed a grin.

"Well, call them off, I'm back."

After Julia dried him and found his wrapper, he told her that on Wednesday Henry had telephoned he was sick. He said when the cab had dropped him off at Henry's apartment, he'd walked up the path, past the twice-cut redwood tree, and somebody had slugged him on the head.

He told Julia that he would eat a little soup or something, but then he must go see what happened to Henry. She argued with him to go to bed, but he dressed and drove away. She probably thought he'd been drunk. His story had not been good; no one had telephoned them Wednesday morning. But she was a kind wife; she hadn't snapped his lie back in his face.

For her sake, he would have to restrain Henry, against his will if necessary. Henry had come within an ace of leaving Julia a widow, expecting a child, without life insurance.

He slammed the brakes, went into a drugstore, and bribed a man to sell him sleeping pills without a prescription. It was possible—probable in fact—they would affect Henry much more than they would him. Hank was usually awake when Henry slept. Henry was always the drunker of the two.

If Henry seemed in a bad mental state, the pills would keep him relaxed and amenable until Hank decided what to do with him. Perhaps he could keep Henry in a lethargic state until his brain more or less gave up. Hank could keep him a drowsy, contented prisoner. Henry might live to be an old, old man that way—no danger of accidents, at least.

Julia and he would be safe. Like any man, he could watch his children grow up, write a novel he was proud of, maybe work into an editorial job on a daily paper. It was not fair that he should die, should lose all that because Henry was cracking up.

He thought, as he rode the elevator to the sixth floor, *Henry would be happier too.* Surely any condition was happier than Henry's present one.

Henry greeted him stiffly. Obviously, he was ashamed. His uneasy smile showed it as he talked. "Wednesday, when I went to class, I made my academic swan song. Feeling quite confident, I spoke in a humorous vein… until I realized they weren't laughing with me. They were laughing at me. I wasn't repressing my liquid courage as well as I imagined.

"I grew angry, ill, and left the hall precipitously. Afterward, when I was able to drive away, I forgot all about you. I finally remembered, several hundred miles from here, but thought I'd let you sleep for a day or two, perhaps removing some of my own tension. It did at first— I felt less depressed than I have in months. But as you see, here I am before you, putrefied."

Hank winced at this. But he knew he'd give him another chance. "I don't bear you any grudge, Henry. If it wasn't for Julia, we could go out and get lunch together. What you should do is—"

"Listen to him," said Henry, humorlessly. "HE doesn't bear me any grudge. He steals my only sweetheart. Because of him, I'm that drunk old Diddoh who won't be back next term. So *he* is generous enough not to bear *me* any grudge."

Henry's voice shrilled, "All I wanted was to be left alone, to marry some nice girl to ease the inevitable death of my mother, but you stole her. You stole part of my brain. Sometimes I wonder if Renworth's convenient death was also your doing . . . and now as I look at your expression, I think it was."

Hank clipped him on the jaw, felt the bright flash in his own consciousness, managed with dim sight and intense concentration to unscrew the bottle and push a pill down the throat of the fallen man. The pill might drug them equally, but there was only one way to find out. He tied Henry's arms spread-eagle across the bed, careful not to stop his circulation, using very loose knots, since his health and Henry's were irrevocably joined.

Henry feebly called for help. What could Hank do but press a pillow over his face? He lifted it every time his own eyes blurred from oxygen starvation of their bimodal brain. Plainly, one pill had not been enough.

"Are you all right, Dr. Diddoh?" A female voice quavered from the hall outside of Henry's apartment.

"Yes, fine, fine," Hank replied in a carefully high-pitched voice.

"Oh, you sound like you're having another of your spells. The doorknob rattled. Hank released the pillow and lunged, falling to his knees, for his own senses were blurring.

"Please, Mrs. Parr, I'm not dressed."

A middle-aged giggle came from the other side of the door: "I'm Miss Taranamack. Mrs. Parr moved out months ago. Now I know you're having one of your spells."

She pushed tentatively against the door. As Hank searched for the lock catch on the unfamiliar hardware, the bed behind him cracked. Over his shoulder he saw Henry sit up, tugging at his still-bound left hand.

Forgetting the door, Hank made an indecisive step toward him.

Henry rolled off the bed and ran to the end of his tether. As he tore his wrist free, he looked toward the tall floor-to-ceiling window.

Hank plunged there ahead of him. Much the stronger, he shoved Henry back over the coffee table, the scream of the woman dinning in his ears. She clawed him as he moved after Henry, who thudded off the end of the table and regained his feet, clutching his prized malachite vase by the neck.

Henry again ran at the window. As Hank lunged to intercept him, the woman, imagining she was defending poor Dr. Diddoh from a madman, caught Hank by the belt. His knee gave way and his finger grazed helplessly across Henry Diddoh's hip.

To Hank, it seemed Henry was in slow motion. Henry fisted his vase through the glass, then his arm, shoulders, and head struck the great outward cracking rectangle with a spray of glass. His body arched through, bent knees followed by his feet tipping up and out of sight. Henry Diddoh was gone from the room loud with the woman's shrieks.

In the double heartbeat that remained, Hank took a forward step and raised his knee to begin another. His thought was: toward the window, out; autopsy would be a matter of quick distaste and he'd be buried a man, a husband dead.

As the jagged frame of broken glass gaped at the sky, Henry, via gravity obliterated his and Hank's consciousness simultaneously.

According to ancient history, a man told to run at the moment a Samurai headsman's sword swung at his head could still run—his body obeying, despite a severed brain.

The cadaver had momentum in its favor.

TEN ROUNDS FOR THE
ALL-TIME CHAMP

Written in St. Augustine FL, 1951-52
Setting: A Late 1940s Boxing Ring

Everything goes slow motion the day of a fight. I notice little details, even before a charity bout.

At weigh-in, they say "Shake hands with the champ," and I notice five, six camera yaks I've never seen before. Country, with bowl-head haircuts, pants don't break on their shoe-tops, one still with a price tag on his coat. They're fumbling speed graphics as if box brownies are what they usually shoot with. But their faces don't spell country; they are sharpy, smoothy, jokes-on-you.

I look at Herky and notice purple scars crinkling around his eyes as I let him shake my hand. I hear one of the telly crankers whisper, "I bet he wishes he was a time-traveler right now. He would sure travel away from this fight," and another says, "he's bald enough for one," and a moth flaps between us.

As I squeeze the knobby-healed bones in Herky's hand, his liver-lips grin at me but I hear him belch a little bubble. I know he's scared. He's scared alright, because when he tries to say something that will make me like him better—how swell it is of me to appear with him in an easy ole exhibition bout—he stammers like when he was my sparring partner. Back then he'd backpedal when he shoulda been leading, and Manny would yell at him to slow down and fight. He's scared all right. When a flashbulb goes off, his whole face blinks.

He is as bald as that time-traveler whose wig blew off.

Poor old Herky. I give the telly my Champion-of-the-World smile from a three-quarter profile. I turn full-face and some feeb asks me again if my weight is right, if I'm "ready."

That makes it easy to smile. I almost laugh—I'd be "ready" for old Canvasback Herky even with my hand broke and my belly hanging as far over my trunks as Herky's.

I'm careful not to look at him because I can't put him away quick and easy, the way he'd like. This is a thirty-bucks-a-ringside Milk Fund go, so the suckers got to see blood. Since they know this is not a box-fight but a slaughter, the audience will boo and yell "Cheese Champ" unless I show them Herky's blood.

The *Times and Herald* compares me to Louis and Dempsey, so I can't afford to get gentle, even for a charity bout. There are no good fighters left for me to look good against, so I've got to look special good against the stumble-bums if they're going to admit I could have cooled either Louis or Dempsey.

I could have. I've seen their old fight pictures. I have my moves all figured out. Someday, even Eebee Fine at the *Daily News* will admit I could have done it.

It's pretty near fight time as I'm sitting on the table with gloves on, popping flies between them that Eddie shoos my way with a towel. I got a tickle in my nose because he's shooing dust at me too from stacks of old newspapers on the floor.

This isn't really a dressing room. It's an office because this auditorium was not meant for boxing. It's a dump, but I'm not sore about it anymore. Manny says the auditorium is packed, fifteen thousand when the papers only predicted five, so I must be pretty good if fifteen thousand paid to watch me work over an old lump-ear like Herky. The public is not so dumb as Eebee Fine.

And Herky's dressing room is worse than mine. It's the ladies' can. Manny says when he went to see if Herky was still breathing, he could hardly see him, it was so dark, one little bulb, no window, and they've got to keep the door shut.

"Slap him for six like I told you," he says. "Then if the press guys look ripe, I'll tell you to nail him."

"Manny," I say, "those fifteen thousand people don't sound right." They're noisy and some are booing the prelim, but I've listened to a lot of crowds. They don't sound right to me.

"Yeah, they don't like those middleweights in there, and they'll be set to work you over too. Try to open up his eye in the first round, overhand—the way you did in Baltimore."

But they don't sound like they're paying attention to the prelim. It sounds like the crowd seven years ago when I met Gargan for the crown, excited for a real fight.

I duck my head at Manny, slide off the table, and begin loosing up my shoulders. Manny hasn't got that crowd figured right.

I hear Ira, the announcer. But that doesn't sound like Ira. I expect the pug with the gray sweatshirt to hammer on my door soon.

It's slow motion just before a fight, so I have time to squat by the dusty newspapers and look at an old picture of myself. COULD BUTCHER HAGEN HAVE TAKEN DEMPSEY?

Since the writer is Eebee Fine, he says "NO!" He says I fight like a fiddler crab, with my chin bumping my knees. He says great fighters stand up when they fight. But I'll bet he's never been hit in the belly till he puked. And anyway, Manny says I'm a natural crouch fighter.

With my gloves I push over pages and see a picture of a big cop with a sad little man in one hand and a wig in the other. TIME-TRAVELER APPREHENDED IN THE

METROPOLITAN MUSEUM. I wonder—why do those travelers always lose their hair?

That traveler claimed he was an art history professor looking at Michelangelo stuff destroyed during the war—that he wanted to go back in time to the Renan-something to meet the guy firsthand. He said the new law against time-travelers or anybody without a proper ID card and birth certificate is reactionary, even for our time. He said we're not interesting anyway because we're too near his present time and too stupid in human relations to be worth warning.

A second picture showed him sitting in the air with a sour-grapes expression on his face and cops standing around to make sure he disappeared.

The door bangs open. The pug in the sweatshirt croaks, "This is it, Champ," like he's on television or something. Then he relaxes. "Hey you mugs, they just caught *another* time-traveler. Somebody asked him who won the main event and, can you gig this, he said he hasn't found out yet—that's what he's here to see." We all laugh.

Manny follows him down the aisle, pushing through standees. Eddie grins at me and picks up the satchel, and I follow him. It's an overflow crowd, jabbering and waving at each other like this is an important fight and they have lots of money down. Sugar-Boy follows me, so close he steps on my heel, which is bad luck. I turn my head to make a crack and ram into Eddie, who has stopped.

Cops bump up the aisle, dragging a guy with a wig in his hand, the time-traveler, who blinks like they've knocked off his glasses, yelling about his ticket being as good as anybody's. He sees me and stops yelling, closes his mouth, and stares at me like he's a good fan, like it's an honor to be dragged past Butcher Hagen.

That's proof to me that I go down big in sports history. I'll tell Eebee Fine that, after the fight.

The crowd goes crazy. I wave my gloves above my head, but they're not paying any attention to me. They're looking at the ring, where Herky's purple bathrobe with the cowl is just ducking beneath between the ropes. I can't see who they're looking at. They're yelling for some general or telly star, probably. But the announcer, who is not Ira, doesn't invite anyone else up. He introduces Herky but gets his name wrong.

He is some stupid announcer I've never seen before.

"Ladies and gentlemen, due to sudden illness, that great heavy-weight, Herkimer Jones, is unable to…" laughter drowns him out, "…that brilliant prospect…"

More laughter. I don't quite catch the name, Baylor or Taylor or something.

The cowl and robe come off. It's not Herky. No belly on this mug. He has red bushy hair and white shoulders with muscles like baseballs on the ends. A line of black hair runs down his big, shiny, white chest, marking into Herky's purple trunks. The stranger curls his glove against his hip, like he's afraid Herky's trunks will slide off. He grins at the crowd. Believe it or not, his rubber mouthpiece is baby blue.

They say he's a "prospect," but when I push through the ropes, I see his face has been in fights before. He's at least as old as I am. His nose is like a pimple, and half of one black eyebrow is gone.

While Manny scurries to the Commissioner, the announcer with too-short tuxedo pants introduces me. The crowd gives me a good hand, but maybe not so good as that redhead got, which makes me sore. He's only a lump-ear from the sticks. I've never even heard of the guy.

He could be only a carnival fighter, but for some reason they like him. Crowds are screwy; most crowds would be booing over the switch. This crowd hasn't done anything right yet. They look all hepped up and happy.

Down over the ring apron I see some familiar faces. Hytower of *The Times* looks goof-eyed over the switch; he pushes his hat so far back on his head it falls off while I watch. He doesn't notice that, for now he's typing like mad, and so is Eebee Fine.

Those hick reporters who were at weigh-in are sitting in a row, grinning like their faces will split. I get the smell that this redhead is a hometown boy, and somebody has put lettuce on Herky's pink palm. Maybe the idea is for country boy to last enough rounds with The Champ so they can write later how he pretty near massacres me, until I land a lucky punch.

"The Commissioner says go ahead," Manny says as I stretch on the corner ropes. "The auditorium manager must have dug this bum up when her kid got sick, and it's too late to do anything about it now."

"Shall I end it quick?"

"No, stay with the plan we had for Herky."

In the center, we meet with the ref, the same old ref, Rudy, slinging the same old bull. Rudy grins at me: a make-the-best-of-it grin. The redhead nods pleasantly, as if to say: You may be Champ, but to me you're just another fighter. He may be a hayseed, but he has a lot of ring poise. I duck my head at him, very polite, laughing inside because Redhead will be another knee-knocker after I bore into that white chest a couple of times. We return to our corners.

Manny says, "Don't push this guy too hard. If he falls over his own feet, you can't look good no matter how hard you bounce him later."

"What if the crowd starts laughing?"

"Champ, if it gets too funny, I'll tell you to end it quick. But don't you clown. Remember what I told you about not leaving your mouth open; those telly cameras are on you every minute. Now go chase him."

Round One

I'm up with the bell and Manny's slap on the butt, out fast. It's an excited crowd. My legs are springy before a noisy crowd, no matter who I'm fighting. I figure this is a swell chance to show Eebee Fine I'm not just a mauler.

Standing straighter than I would against a good fighter, we exchange jabs. I telescope my right without throwing it, not much, just enough to test his reflexes. His open glove covers fast. He would have picked it off.

As I work him toward his corner, he's full of early-round bounce, waggling his shoulders, faking with his feet and head, grinning around his blue mouthpiece. But he's not clowning-scared. I find that out when he counters my left, flat-footed with weight behind his, snapping my head back. He follows in with a right that I block.

My left tags him loud, but he hangs in there and lifts a right out of nowhere as we bump apart, so quick I surprise myself how neatly I deflect it. It skids my right cheek, and I tie him up again, break before Rudy can move in, then flick one leaving him with a taste of leather in his mouth.

To my surprise, he closes on me, stabbing lefts, takes my straight-from-the-shoulder left and sledgehammers me in the ribs. A couple of those, and I'm playing fiddler crab, blocking his hooks, bobbing under his jabs, moving in again, the only way for me to fight him. Up straight, he had me off balance. I'm a natural crouch fighter.

I have him backing and sidestepping at the bell.

"What were you trying to be at the beginning?" Manny laughs, "Ray Robinson?" He squeezes the back of my neck. "Watch out for this guy; he's tricky on his feet. He can make you look clumsy. He's no carnival bum."

That's no lie.

Round Two

In the second, he plants a string of solid lefts when I'm coming in. Whenever I land on him, he's going away. My eyes sting from cigar smoke.

"You're not pushing him enough," Manny says. "Start catching him with your right. I'll bet he's got more points so far than you have. Be aggressive with this boy."

What does he think I'm trying to be? I'm chasing that guy all over the ring.

Round Three

As I barrel into him, he drives out a fast right that scrubs skin off my ear as I twitch away from it. For an instant I think I have him as I roundhouse, but he's too quick, rolling away so we end up breathing hard in a clinch where I have the better of it. He sure isn't afraid to take chances.

It comes to me this mug is winning a moral victory, making me look like molasses in January. Already he's earned himself a place among the so-called contenders. I'll have to put him away before the sixth if they are going to keep calling me greater than Louis.

"Use your right," Manny gasps. "He can't have much of a punch, or he'd already be in the bigtime. Forget our plan for Herky! Nail him anytime you can."

Easy to say.

Round Four

He's cute, easing off, waiting for me to try something risky, waiting his right glove. His left is a blur at my eyes, his chest big, white, shiny, moving around.

The crowd complains. I remind myself he has nothing in his gloves but hands.

What are they writing at ringside? I lose my temper and try to smash my big one through a small opening. As it deflects over his shoulder, I go blind. I can't even feel where his right-counter hit me.

I finally see the ref's hand pumping up and down, but the crowd is roaring so loud I can't hear what the count is. I get up off my knees and along the ropes doing the wobbly, covering like I haven't covered since Golden Gloves. Now Eebee Fine and the hick reporters must be happy. I want to yell and spit out my mouthpiece, I'm so mad. But I've been around long enough not to try to straighten and throw one. You get so you know when the bell is coming, and anyway my gloves are too heavy.

"Take it easy," Manny wheezes as I spit in the bucket. "We got a Garden Fight in three weeks. Let him open the next round."

I wonder if Manny is happy too. If Redhead takes this go, the return match, a title bout, will flood the telly channels. We'll all grow very, very rich but I won't be the greatest heavyweight of all time. I'll just be one of the bums after tonight unless I blotto this bushleaguer.

Round Five

I wrestle him in the fifth with the crowd yelling because they want to see my blood, something new in these parts. I hold him like a sweetheart and make Rudy the ref most unhappy. The crowd yells—it's unhappy too. But I'm waiting for my legs to firm up. Although Redhead starts my ears ringing, I survive the round pretty well.

Flopping a towel before my face, Manny screams so I can hear him: "You tied him up good. This next round too!"

I wonder if Manny wants me to lose this fight. He's talking that way.

Round Six

Redhead is after me fast, but jabby. His manager must have told him "for god's sake stay out of that bear hug." When I stand up to him, pick off his right with my open glove and move in, he backpedals faster than in earlier rounds. I wait for him. The decision is already lost. It's got to be a sudden rush and a knockout, so I'm saving myself, even if voices are squalling that I'm yellow.

He goes around me like Indians around Custer. He tries a few flurries, but I've been in the ring a long time. My only solid right hand of the round splits his cheek over the bone and blood spreads down his cheek.

Guys with thin, white skins split easy, Manny tells me, as he doctors me up too. "Keep after that cheek. We may have a TKO by the tenth." He looks happy—in a shebang like this he can't lose.

But a technical knockout from a cut won't save my reputation. If I'm the greatest fighter of all time, I need to canvas him for ten. But that's still not happening.

Round Seven

I'm moving slowly, as if my legs are gone. But Redhead wants me to do the risking. He fences, his guard high up around his face, and won't come in. He'll be happy with a decision, his style says.

I turn until he's close to the ropes, then charge under his gloves, slamming both hands to the body. He seems to be thinking so much about his cheek he's slow at bringing his guard down. I double him over my shoulder before he can uppercut me and butt him along the ropes with the boom of the crowd in my ears. He's holding on, and I'm trying to hammer through. But he twists as I drive right; my arm scrapes over the rope as I thud on one knee. I'm up quick and after him, but he's still the dancer. He coughs and gags as I follow him, his stomach and chest blotched red. The crowd yells for the kill. But Redhead sidesteps, catches me wide open with a right I should have blocked, splatting out my mouthpiece, tipping me off balance and following with a straight left to the button.

I lurch back three steps to keep from falling, duck under his looping right and plant mine in his oncoming stomach. His left drives my cheek into my teeth. He misses with his right uppercut; I beat him to the punch. He lunges sideways, off-balance, with me following, drooling blood as I come.

The bell ends that.

"For Pete's sake," Manny yells, "work on his cheek, just snipe at his cheek! You got a Garden Fight coming up."

Eddie elbows my manager aside and inserts a new, cool mouthpiece.

Round Eight

This round, I go hunting. This is a funny crowd; yelling equally for either man.

Now I'm the favorite. I chase the redhead, but he's mad. He doesn't like to give ground. Jabbing at my eyes, he bluffs with his right, sidesteps, bangs me on the ear. I hurt him in that last round. Apparently, he has pride, as if he's a champion too—for he rushes, catching me by surprise and probably his manager too.

Off-balance, I'm his punching bag. He's getting uppercuts under my crotch as I back into the ropes. The touch of the ropes is like a sprayer, and I drive forward.

I hear a countdown at six but am up and backing away by nine, so we're at it again. A close call. He rushes me so fast his right punch misses, looping clear around my neck. We wrestle chest-to-chest in the long moment before the bell.

Round Nine

"For Pete's sake!" That's all Manny says as I open my mouth and let the tomato juice drain into the bucket, while Eddie slits the puff under my eye. Sugar-Boy holds my head steady, groaning for both of us until Eddie finishes with the razor. It will hurt later, but I don't want to lose a peeper.

The faraway voice of Manny says something again about a Garden Fight as they pull the stool from under me. I'm out again following the red-chested man, slaps of his left echoing through my head. But I'm interested in his bulls-head right and the tricky pattern of his feet. I stop, he stops. I move forward, he moves back. There's only this round, then the tenth to catch him in.

I straighten up the way I fought in the first round. This is just a bluff; I want to suck him at me. He sucks all right!

I rest until a count of seven. Getting up is much harder than I thought it would be. At the count of nine, he's out of his neutral corner. Rudy should have held him back a sec or two. He's after me with both hands, very loud against my forearms and ears.

Very good, I think, just the way I wanted it. I'll catch you coming in. Watching his feet, I hook a left that's like lifting a barbell with heavyweight Galento hanging on my arm. As my eyes move up his chest, the lights flicker. This is a lousy place for a fight, no air-conditioning, lousy lights.

At the count of four, I roll over on my stomach. Pushing myself up at eight, I climb back into the ropes, making like a crab. He makes the mistake of rushing me too fast, and I get my arms around his waist. The canvas is no good; it's slippery. A couple taps on the head, and I slip. He pulls away and I land on my knees, staring at the catsup my nose left on his pink and white chest.

When I get up, he isn't in front of me, so I know the bell has rung. I walk to my corner, but Redhead is sitting in it. I stagger to the corner Manny and my seconds beckon me to.

Rudy comes over to ask if I'm all right. I nod my head and shove Manny away.

Round Ten

Redhead gets off his stool, so I come out and touch gloves with him for the last round.

As I move in on him, it's easier to think—to consider all the angles, to wonder where this guy came from. He sure is a ringer. If I'd known I was fighting a boxer instead of Herky, I'd have trained down a little finer.

But it only takes one punch, says the part of me watching the fight. The thinking part is glad it isn't in on the fighting now because that redhead is really dishing it out with both hands. Only one punch, I think.

I shake my head, realize I'm sitting in my corner waiting for the next one, figuring out how I will bicycle, then rush and trap him in a corner. But then I notice the ring is filling up with people. I walk toward them so the announcer can raise my hand, for the round has stopped so suddenly I figure I must have knocked him out, strictly one punch. My gloves have already been cut off.

Redhead comes across and shakes my hand, saying, "You were my hero when I was a kid." What? We looked the same age. I must have knocked him punchy.

The microphone pushes at me. I say, "Great fight. Hope to schedule him a title go. He's a great prospect."

At this, all the guys in hick suits grin. The announcer looks embarrassed and mumbles something about Double-Champ Taylor fighting this guy for charity and not fighting anymore around here.

The crowd is carrying Redhead toward Herky's dressing room on their shoulders, and Sugar-Boy's face is turned up at me, crying.

Not until then does it soak into me that I didn't win.

A decision—the AP cards it as six rounds for Taylor, two for me, two even. It's the first fight I've lost since turning pro eleven years ago.

Some writers I know gather around me while part of the crowd struggles up the main aisles. But a big ocean of people follows Redhead into his dressing room. Never have I seen so many follow a fighter, all whooping like he's daily-double come home.

They pour into his dressing room, the ladies' can, like the Mississippi River. They jam around the little door as the center of the crowd pours into that little dressing room. I think they must be trampling others to death in there, piling 'em up like sugar sacks in a freight car.

Going up the near-deserted aisle with Eddie and Sugar-Boy, I look back. The crowd is still forcing itself through that small opening—thousands laughing and punching each other like this Taylor is an old buddy and his win was what they figured.

"Double-Champ, Double-Champ," they yell as they push their way into that little dressing room until it is impossible. There's no way out—no other doors or windows.

Next day, Eebee Fine would write that it seemed near two-thirds of the auditorium crowd, ten thousand people, poured into Herky's dressing room—a room only twenty by twenty with a low ceiling. But they poured through the door until they all disappeared, then the door closed after the last of them.

Then the auditorium had quieted, except for a few kids running up and down the aisle, picking up wigs and sailing them toward the ring. Manny had kicked more wigs out of the way, limping and jumping up the aisle with his sleeve pulled off his coat, his expression enough to scare a mad dog.

I see there will be no rematch.
"Well," I say, not sadly for the pains haven't started yet. "I'm sort of relieved I wasn't beat by what Eebee Fine calls a 'contemporary bum.' That sleeper right hand of his will give Joe Louis plenty trouble."

"Dempsey too," says Eddie.

"Poor ole Jack Johnson," sighs Sugar-Boy.

WE SPECIALISTS

Written in Santa Barbara, CA in 1967
Setting: Any Large City in the Future

Intruding from far behind Kitty G3 on the pedestrian mall, shrieks rose in pitch, then diminished in volume as something metallic hammered onto the pavement.

Kitty G3 glanced back through the hurrying-home-from-work crowd bumping her along the northbound pedestrian lane. She glimpsed a white coat illegally halted in the pedestrian intersection. A man's white sleeve violently rose upward, his hand holding a steel pipe glinting in the red afternoon sunlight. He struck down at a huddled body.

Disgustedly, Kitty G3 saw how inconsiderately the woman's body and the man in the white coat impeded pedestrian traffic. She glanced at the sky.

Typically, whenever one was needed, a Traffic Flow Specialist appeared overhead. Helplessly, Kitty G3 hurried on, anxious not to impede pedestrian traffic herself. Her tight shoes were killing her, but she couldn't stop until she reached the monorail waiting zone.

There was no place to sit, with a solid mass of people waiting in front of her for the next monocar. Her identity badge: Bank Teller: Deposits Only Specialist, entitled her to this nightly commute to her cute bachelorette apartment. That identity badge also gave her the reassurance of knowing exactly who she was and assured her of public services as long as she lived.

Crowding ahead of her, a bald man holding a newspaper displayed on his chest his more impressive identity badge: Accountant: Debits Only Specialist.

Kitty G3 heard another shriek, close behind her. She turned and saw the same young man in the white coat bending down as he clubbed another woman. Because this well-dressed matron had fallen face downward, her identity badge was not visible. Each time the steel pipe smacked against the back of her head, the crowd moved further away from the spattering blood.

With his newspaper, the Accountant: Debits Only Specialist shielded his suit, carefully turning his head aside so that he couldn't be accused of staring. Kitty G3 looked away. No police or medical or mortuary specialist appropriate to the situation had stepped from the crowd, and Kitty G3 made the mistake of peeking again.

As the young man straightened, his white coat speckled with blood, Kitty G3 was shocked to see he wasn't wearing any identity badge at all. Embarrassed, she looked away. Too late. She realized he'd seen her staring at his blank chest, his bare, barren chest with no identity badge at all.

She felt her body quivering, perhaps even a perverse thrill. She'd never before seen a grown man not wearing any identity badge at all. When her former fiancé used to slip into her apartment, both of them morally would turn away while undressing in order to securely tape their identity badges to their bodies. Now she wondered if all men really needed to wear their identity badges in order to be able to …

The blow startled her, numbing her shoulder and whole left arm. She couldn't raise it as she staggered away from the upraised pipe with the man's distraught face behind. She would have screamed for help, but the badges of the those around her showed them as specialists in office work, accountancy, truck driving, karate— none of them appropriate to a specialized police situation.

She lurched into the left-turn pedestrian lane and darted across the opposing lane, losing one shoe. Her left arm swung heavily, numb. She fled through the revolving glass door of the nearest store.

"Help!" she blurted. "Someone should report a man who isn't —" Her face burned with embarrassment. "…wearing any identity badge at all. He tried to —"

A mustachioed clerk delicately placed a martini glass on a shimmering pyramid of glasses and peered through them at her identity badge. His identity badge limited him to Glassware Salesman, Martini Glass Specialist. He smiled helplessly. "Dear, let me sell you a quarter dozen martini glasses instead."

The young man in the white coat breathed heavily behind her. Kitty G3 turned to stare at him. He raised that stainless-steel pipe as it dribbled the last woman's blood down onto his knuckles. As she backed up, past trembling tiers of martini glasses, the Martini Glass Specialist shrieked: "Please, no family quarrels in glassware."

"Help!" Kitty G3 looked frantically for an appropriate police specialist in the store. She saw a plexiglass miniphone booth as she dodged a blow. Falling martini glasses tinkled.

"Sir, don't beat your wife in here, sir, not even a stranger," the Glassware Salesman Martini Glass Specialist reasoned from a safe distance, "…because each glass is balanced on another; if one falls, we all fall. If one crashes, we all crash. Young lady, obviously you have no intention of purchasing glassware. Return to the pedestrian mall where you belong. I can assure you he will follow. Won't you, sir?"

With a clang, the pipe fell to the artificial marble floor. The young man sobbed, then laughed breathlessly. His bloody hand rose to the empty space on his white coat to leave a red handprint where his identity badge was not. Beside his brown shoe, his stained steel pipe was threaded at one end. It must have been unscrewed from some sort of specialized equipment, Kitty G3 thought vaguely, as she backed into the miniphone booth.

Whirling, she pressed her identity badge against the activator grid.

"Your friendly police department," the recorded desk sergeant's voice oozed years of public relations, "is delighted to receive your call and something already is being done about whatever you wish to report. Please identify…"

"Help! He isn't wearing any identity badge at all."

"For cases of indecent exposure, an appropriate re-identity specialist will be sent."

"No. Wrong specialist." She gasped as the steel pipe slammed against her spine. "Hitting me!"

"The appropriate Family Quarrel Specialist will be…"

"No. Wrong specialist. Stranger hitting me. God. Hurts. Killing me!"

"Data correlation and deduction!" The telephone buzzed triumphantly. "Sir or Madam, your friendly police department has analyzed your last statement, and our most appropriate police specialist already has been sent."

Outside the glass store door, the sparrow-quick police copter clanged down from heaven. The steel pipe echoed through her skull. She writhed on the artificial marble floor with both broken arms, unable to shield her eyes. The pipe struck again. Her eyes blinked.

Embarrassed, the appropriately shrewd-looking police specialist looked down at her vanishing face. He stood, not moving, waiting, as both of Kitty G3's retinas were detached by the blows.

But as her shrieks faded, before being beaten blind, she'd glimpsed the police man's identity badge and empathetically understood why he couldn't help her.

His badge read: Homicide Specialist.

PART 2: STRANGE ENCOUNTERS ON EARTH

GREMMIE'S REEF

Written in 1964
A Surfer Story, set on Pacific coast, somewhere
near Santa Barbara, California
Previously in IF Worlds of Science Fiction, October 1964

Dangerously overbalanced by his long fire engine-red surfboard, a young teen, Ted, tried to climb down the cliff.

White gulls ballooned in the updraft of wind against the dusty white cliff. He slipped. His skinny feet scurried for footholds down the crumbling chalk. The high wind of the Pacific Ocean knifed his wide eyes, and the hissing updraft lifted his red surfboard like a wing in his arms. Staggering high above the high-tide surf, he fell.

"The same to you!" Ted spat chalk and sand and the taste of blood. With stinging knees he knelt on the narrow beach beside his red surfboard, fingering the chalk-streaked dents. "You dinged my board too!"

The sea wind ruffled his thick brown thatch of hair. On top of his bent head, his fluttering mop glowed yellow from his mother's peroxide bottle, junior high school style. In the dazzling beach sunlight he wore a halo. But his stubborn lower lip was bleeding as he scowled down at the damage to his board.

Behind his back, the surface of the ocean writhed. A gleaming area as large as a football field bulged the surface, quivering, and sank down a few feet, forming rows of swells in deep water where no swells should be. The tide was going down, and low tide would expose it. It looked almost like the flank of a large animal.

As if any animal—any Earthly animal—were that bright purple color.

Turning, Ted glared at the shore-break, the steep waves breaking unrideably close upon the sand, and looked no further out. His more alert older brother would have noticed the disturbed water out there where the gulls were wheeling and crying. But the boy scowled at his damaged surfboard again. "Crumby board! If I try to ride these waves, probably break in half."

The surfboard already was a patchwork of fiberglass-cloth repairs disguised with red paint. It was his brother's old board, scarred from heroic wipe-outs on the rocks at Hammond's Reef, spectacular clobberings at Rincon Point, collisions at Huntington Beach concrete pier, and other great surfing spots where his brother David wouldn't take him.

His famous brother would raise his eyebrows in mock amazement that he, Ted, would even ask to tag along. "Decision negative." His head-shaking brother was a mighty SENIOR, a magnificent suntan-lotion bronze with ooh-ah muscles from years of paddling surfboards, and a modest grin.

To make it worse, his brother was an eager-beaver brain who got all "As" last semester, a member of the —bugles, please—California Scholastic Federation. Worse still, his brother had poked thermometers into sea anemones and won First Prize at the Science Fair. He got his picture in the newspaper.

Now, instead of watching television like a normal guy, his brother studied right through Midnight Movie. His brother was praying for a scholarship to Stanford to study marine biology. His brother was sweating out the National Scholarship Tests. David had developed a temper like a hand grenade. Groaning, he would now permit himself only two hours of surfing per week. During those two hours—

"Go home!" his brother would yell when Ted followed David's surfing club to the beach. "Go home! You can't surf. These waves are too big. You'll get clobbered. And don't break any bottles on the beach, you gremmie!"

His brother's surfing buddies would laugh like crazy.

"I am not a gremmie."

Alone now beneath the chalk cliff, the boy glared seaward at the unrideable five-foot high shore break.

These waves crashed straight down with popping noises. Their white soup tumbled straight in over the high-tide sand. He knew that the straight shape of the beach and deep water directly offshore made the place impossible for surfing. Surfers never came here, so he could practice stupidly riding the surf all day without anybody laughing at him. He waxed his board. He dragged it into the knee-deep froth. He still did not notice what had happened out in deep water.

Whirling, he vaulted into his board. As he tried to stand, his board shot out from under him like a cake of soap. He fell backward, plopping awkwardly in the shallows. He sprang up, glancing guiltily at the cliff-top. There was no one to witness his embarrassment. Dripping, he chased after his board. The wind turned icy.

The next try, the board twisted beneath his feet like a treacherous snake. He fell sideways, flailing the air with one arm, ending up with an earful of sand. The tide was going down and he kept falling off his board, trying to stand up on it, falling off again, trying to stand again, with endless determination.

His scoutmaster had described him in this way: "Most single-minded kid I ever saw. Spends all day trying to tie one knot. Also most unobservant. Lucky we don't live in Africa. I'd tell him to pitch his tent between four tree trunks, and he'd pitch it underneath an elephant. That kid's narrow eyes would never even notice."

Lower lip thrust out, when Ted tried the soup again, he stood up all the way to the beach—almost. Toppling forward, he leaped, landing deftly on his feet, and his board whacked him across the shins angrily.

"I'll show him! I can too surf! Some day—great big eight-foot walls breaking on Hammond's Reef —when my crumby brother chickens, I'll ride one. I will! Or a tube, a really big tube breaking along the Santa Barbara sandspit— ten feet high," he lapsed into pure fantasy, "…twenty feet high at the Banzai Pipeline in Hawaii."

All this time the tide was going down.

Staring out at the vast Pacific, Ted blinked.

Way out there, shimmering circular bulges rose in the water as if swells were passing over a submerged reef.

"There's no reef out there!"

As he watched, one of the swells creamed over, at least two hundred yards from shore, an easy downpouring like Waikiki.

"Like wow!" He could hardly believe it. His brother had taken him spearfishing out there, sloshing around with fins and masks, and there hadn't been any reef. The water had been twenty feet deep with dark beds of pebbles and weeds and light patches of sand—nothing to make those perfect surfing waves build up.

Why now?

"Don't ask questions," he whispered his junior high school motto: "just have fun, man!"

Paddling out with hurried strokes, as if the reef would swim away or something, Ted discovered it was a heck of a long way out there. Those waves were big, with white teeth.

"Worse can do—is clobber me," he gasped, paddling harder.

Ahead of him a glassy swell stood up, with flashing schools of anchovies silhouetted above his head. And up.

His board flopped safely over its unbroken crest. He paddled beyond the break and came about. The reef seemed to cover as much space as a football field with an upward bulge near the fifty-yard line.

Vaguely, briefly, he imagined some kind of sand pile down there. But deep thinking was something he didn't fuss with. That was his brother's department. His sunburned nose wrinkling, Ted grinned with excitement. Never had he tried to catch a wave as big as the monster swell that was building up over the reef and gliding toward him.

"No questions," he thought, paddling like mad to stay ahead, to catch the curl or be cleaned up. "Just got to surf, man." He glanced back blurry eyed, as the swell loomed then heaved under him. Like an elevator it lifted his board, and the nose of his surfboard lunged out over nothingness. In that instant of truth, he didn't chicken, didn't backwater, didn't ask questions. "Yeeoww!"

His mischievously grinning junior high science teacher had written on the blackboard: 'In the universe of men and oceans, planets and space, there are galaxies of *answers* so amazing we don't even know their *questions*.'

"Give us—a new and astounding question—uh—Ted."

"Huh?" Ted had blushed, hot faced, the schoolroom dim to his eyes because he'd been staring out the window. He'd scratched his T-shirt with embarrassment. He hadn't known what to answer. A *questioner* he didn't want to be. All he wanted to be was a surfer—the greatest surfer who ever lived!

"Yee-oww-eeeee!" Triumphantly shouting, he stood erect upon his surfboard. His surfboard seemed to grow eyes and a brain, a built-in guidance system, as it slid down the face of the wave, a perfect right-slide away from the bulging center of the reef. "I am an eagle!"

In his self-imposed ignorance, Ted didn't even know this surfer shout had originated from the excited word-signals of an early Russian cosmonaut, circling the earth.

The ocean spray whirled past his triumphant face. Away from the influence of the reef, the wave smoothed out and his board slowed. Ted shuffled backward, stalling his surfboard and swinging its nose seaward over the declining hump of the swell without falling off. He dropped to his knees, paddling back toward the wonderful new reef, grinning and wheezing with exertion.

"Man, if my big-wheel brother saw that great ride — me—his eyeballs would drop out!"

His brother's eyeballs would have become somewhat distended if he had taken a close look at the reef. But even Ted's brother would not have been able to ask the inspired question, the astounding question which could lead to an answer, an explanation of the reef. The key question was too wild:

What is the connection between the appearance of this reef and the sudden disappearance back in 1964 of our Mariner IX space probe?

If asked, Ted would have guessed a Mariner was a— uh—not a sailor—a satellite maybe? His brother would have described it as a deep space probe physically resembling a miniature oil derrick and programmed to orbit a neighboring planet. At least Mariner IX was. It also could react to command signals from Earth, radioing back information its sensors—its primitive electrical nervous system—had collected. Its behavior patterns were far less complicated and less flexible than a rat's. In this respect, Ted's brother would have compared it to an amoeba.

A glittering mass of water curled high above the reef, a hollowed wave that made Ted shout with joy: "A tube, a real tube!"

There couldn't be much water over the center of the reef to make such a beautiful tube. The tide was going down, he thought. Hurriedly, he positioned his board across the center of the reef when the wave came. He wanted to try to go right through the next tube the way big guys did in surfing movies in Hawaii. His eyes widened. Big swell coming; should he, or shouldn't he?

Ted took a little chicken-hearted stroke. Before he could backwater, his board took off across the face of a wave as if it had a mind of its own, right-sliding down and down until the crest teetered high above him and his board was shooting along the foot of the liquid cliff. His right hand extended as if to hold back the overhanging wave-tube. The crest toppled above his head as he ran toward the nose of his board, trying to increase speed before the tunnel-like wave ate him.

Even his imaginative brother would not have considered that an *answering* space probe would enter Earth's gravitational field. This was five months after Mariner IX unexpectedly went silent, only five months after Mariner XI emitted a last squeak more characteristic of a rat than an amoeba. The embarrassing silence that followed the newspapers had been blamed on another of the long history of short-circuits, electrical malfunctions and battery failures which had plagued the National Aeronautics and Space Administration. Privately, certain ulcerous administrators cursed the day electricity was—uh—invented.

In their tortured imaginations they would have been willing to believe even in an *organic* space probe, if it promised to be free of short-circuits, electrical malfunctions, battery failures and congressional investigating committees. Ted's brother would have laughed: "Impossible! Living protoplasm unshielded can't survive the vacuum and hard radiation of outer space."

The microscopic spore had entered Earth's gravitational field, drifted safely through the Van Allen radiation belt, spiraled inward through the crowding atoms of Earth's upper atmosphere, and settled in the Pacific Ocean.

Its chromosomes had been artificially arranged, programmed so that it would grow in a predetermined pattern. When it was huge enough, its billions of neurons would be able to generate jolts of electricity an electric eel would envy, and no short-circuits as it radioed back information its blind sensors had collected. It was the *answering* space-probe, growing huge as a roof along the ocean floor.

T he nose of Ted's surfboard, pearl-diving, jammed into the reef. His arms spread like wings as he flipped over the nose of his board. The liquid roof caved in.

His knees hit bottom. The blinding wave-surge dragged him along the reef and left him sitting there, exposed. Between swells the reef now had only six inches of water on it.

To his surprise, his knees didn't feel scraped or skinned. Beneath his feet the reef felt rubbery.

As he peered down, he almost imagined he could see the bottom deep beneath him instead of right under his toes as he waded. Characteristically, his eyes narrowed with suspicion, as if he was afraid some big guys, like his brother, were playing a joke on him. But he still thought he could make out blurry beds of pebbles and weeds and light patches of sand, all as dim as if they were twenty feet below his feet. The next wave knocked him rumble-seat over the tea-kettle.

In the deep water inside the reef, wheezing and snorting, Ted dog-paddled toward shore, pursuing his surfboard.

"Clobbered me—but I can really surf!" Ted sloshed excitedly through the shallows after his surfboard, which was cruising upside-down with its skeg-keel in the air like a little sail gleaming purple.

Purple?

"My crumby brother! What'd he do—making my board's skeg turn purple? The nose of his red surfboard, where it stuck in the reef, was stained purple, too. "Doesn't rub off. But I'll twitch him. I'll show him I can really surf, man!"

Dragging his board to the base of the chalk cliff, leaving it there unguarded, a stupid move in any man's language, Ted scrambled up the cliff and hot-footed over the burning concrete sidewalks for five blocks.

"David! David!" he yelled his way through the living room and into his brother's bedroom. "I can surf! I can really surf! You got to see me. Big tubes, I been riding 'em. Really big like Hawa— Leggo me! Ow!"

"Then shut up, you gremmie, when I'm trying to study!" David seemed slightly irritated, like an awakened grizzly bear with his foot caught in a trap and attacked by hornets. "Everybody's bothering me!"

"Please, David, you got to see! Really big surfing waves."

"Shut up. I'll never win a National Merit Scholarship Award with you always bothering me!" David roared, "I've got to study."

"Beautiful surfing waves, David, on a reef like—"

"I'm never going surfing again." David groaned as if he were trying to win an Academy Award.

"*Fantastico* tubes like you never—"

"Get outta here! Get your dirty feet off my rug!"

"Please, David! Just watch me ride one wave, just one wave."

"You stupid crock, even your knees are purple. I said get your dirty purple feet off my rug." David bayoneted him backward off the rug with his hard-pointing karate finger. "You've been wading in athlete's foot medicine. No, you little fiend, you been trampling sea hares. Purple sea slugs to you, you half-pint monster."

"I have not! This purple won't hurt your crumby rug. See, this purple won't rub off," Ted yelled angrily. "All I wanted you to do is watch me ride one wave."

"Shuddup!"

The trigger word, *wave*, seemed to redouble David's fury. Breathing hard, he pinned Ted against the enormous short-wave radio transmitter cabinet. Its remaining knobs and switches felt uncomfortably bumpy against Ted's bare back. The transmitter had been partially dismantled because David had lost his ham radio license. The FCC had taken it away after Federal Communications Commission investigators had discovered it was David who was experimenting on unauthorized wave lengths.

"Just one wave, David," Ted squeaked.

"No! No! No! I am supposed to be studying. I'll never win a scholarship to Stanford now." David's room already was decorated with red and white Stanford pennants covering his butterfly collections, neatly pinned row on row.

His Karate finger jammed deeper into Ted's stomach. "Go away, you little gremmie."

Ted tried to – lunging sideways. His arm slashed into David's twenty-gallon aquarium, tearing the black paper screening.

David yelped with horror. "You've disturbed 'em."
Two eyeless pink things emerged from the muddy tunnels at the bottom of the aquarium, darted about and vanished again.

"How will I win another Science Fair Award with you always bothering my blind gobies!" David was feeding them bait doped with fluorescent dye so that he could watch them in the dark. "Get away from my black light. You're dripping water on it, you crock!" David had caught the gobies, tiny blind fish, by digging up the mud-tunnels of ghost shrimps in a tide pool. In the aquarium he had laid a sheet of glass on the mud, a roof for their tunnels.

In darkness, when David had turned on the ultraviolet fluorescent light, the gobies glowed purple as if they had been dyed. David had color-tagged them so he could watch their movements while the blind gobies thought they were in darkness, invisible. Glowing purple, they wiggled out of the tunnels of their host, the ghost shrimp, to search for more glowing purple food— provided by David, the hard-eyed experimenter.

"Please, David! Just watch me ride one wave across the reef. You won't even have to climb down the cliff."

"What cliff? There's no cliff at Hammond's Reef."

"This is another reef, David. A better reef."

"I have to study. What reef are you talking about?"

Without thinking, Ted blurted the truth: "At the Chalk Cliff."

"The Chalk Cliff?" David roared. "No surfing waves, no reef at the Chalk Cliff. Whatta you mean bothering me? Whatta you mean telling lies? No surfing at the Chalk Cliff. Not even you gremmies go there. The Chalk Cliff! Have a knuckle burger!"

"Oh, David! A reef, a new reef. Don't cork me again, David."

"Then say that you're a dirty lying bothering little gremmie. Go on, say it! There is no reef at the Chalk Cliff."

"But there is a reef. Please, David! A surfers' reef."

"Now you got me so nervous I'll never study again. Everybody bothering me. I've got to get out of here," David groaned. "I'm going to Hammond's Reef."

But when David's 1937 Ford woody station wagon burped to a halt, it was at Chalk Cliff.

"See, David! Look, David, real tubes! Look at 'em building out there on the reef!"

David's Adam's apple jiggled. Speechless, he stood up through the hole in the roof of his woodie. Finally, his voice squeaked with awe and joy. "I'm stoked!"

"A new reef, a phenomenon, an anomaly…" David's voice faded as he whipped his surfboard over the tailgate.

"Cowabunga!" David yelled like a cornball and galloped down the slanting cliff as if he'd turned off the law of gravity.

Like mad, as if he saw his perfect wave coming, David paddled toward the cresting reef.

"Hey, wait, David, wait for me. It was *me* you came to watch ride one…" By the time Ted finished falling down the cliff, his brother was already maneuvering his surfboard to take off into a tube.

Erect, with perfect surfing form, David angled across the face of the wave toward the shallows of the hidden reef. His wave shimmered skyward above his head, rising and hollowing into a translucently green flowing tube.

It was beautiful. David's board hit the invisible reef so hard he ran right off the nose and seemed to be running through the air when he vanished into a wave.

He emerged, crawling eighteen inches above the water, when the wave passed. On all fours, David began thumping the air beneath him, his fists bouncing back as if he was hitting rubber. The next wave buried him.

David reappeared standing on nothing. His raised hands glinted purple as he waded toward shore. Abruptly, he sank as he stepped off the edge of the reef. Sputtering, he swam toward Ted's board.

"Stay away or you'll damage it," David gasped. "Delicate scientific experiment … I'll be famous. Careful scientific investigation." He wallowed hurriedly toward the beach.

"Wait, David! Watch me ride one, just one wave."

But David was retreating rapidly up the cliff.

"Now watch me, David, watch me!" Taking off, sliding away from the center of the reef, Ted rose unsteadily on his board. "Look, David! Look at me ride!"

But David had vanished behind the station wagon.

Without falling off, Ted stalled his board and paddled out again.

"Hey David, watch me this time!"

David plowed down the slanting cliff through rising chalk dust, with some things clutched in his hands. He splashed through the shallows after his capsized board.

"Look at me, David, look at me ride." Ted fell off.

David paddled past him muttering: "Be quiet, delicate scientific tests…"

A heavy ballpeen hammer dangling from one fist, David clambered onto the invisible reef. With the scientific delicacy of a blacksmith, David pounded a huge screwdriver into the reef. There was an electrical crackling.

David rose. Ted glimpsed him rising ten feet above the ocean as the waves rolled back. Then David fell. The water spread bright purple.

With more anger than surprise, Ted witnessed his reef and the protruding handle of David's screwdriver streaking out to sea like a periscope trailing purple foam.

"You ruined my reef! You never even watched me ride one wave!"

To Ted's disappointed yells, David made no reply. David's contorted face seemed purple.

Even when David became the first brilliant purple student to win a National Merit Award Scholarship, he had very little to say. David spent his time scowling at his mirror. Purple?

Now he could *never* go to Stanford. Their colors were red and white.

Skin specialists insisted the purple dye would wear off, but it didn't. Not even sandpaper helped.

Amazingly, David was as popular as ever.

"Put on a gold-colored shirt to go with your cute purple face," David's buxom girlfriend giggled, "and enroll at U.S.C. with me."

The tragedy was Ted.

"Everybody's staring at me." Ted wouldn't go out of the house. "Everybody's laughing at me. I'm not a cow. Everybody's making jokes about a purple cow. Nobody liked me to begin with and now they say I'm a freak. At least you're purple all over, David. I'm all blotchy." He slumped in despair.

In deep water, the gigantic space probe had stopped contracting. It had dissolved the intruding screwdriver. Gradually the probe expanded along the bottom toward shore, huger than ever. As it bulged reef-like toward the surface, gulls whirled above the disturbed water.

With a shriek, a gull veered away as if it had bounced off a plate glass window and crashed into the sea. The gull's sodden breast feathers turned purple. It was dead.

Across the continent at New York's Yankee Stadium, the pitcher let loose the first ball of the World Series.

In the boys' bedroom Ted laughed at the portable TV, frantically twisting the horizontal control knob. There was nothing but a jumble of upward rolling lines and roaring static on every channel.

"Wherever I go!" Ted shrieked. "Static's in here, too, so it isn't just the living room TV. It's everywhere I go. Being purple isn't enough. Now I can't even watch TV!"

In the living room, that TV set shouted clearly: "Strike one!" Its perfect picture showed the batter turning to stare in amazement at the umpire's upraised arm.

David had gone out into the hall. Now as he came back into the living room, the pitcher's intent face freckled with static snow. The picture rolled and David stepped closer to adjust the horizontal control. The pitcher's contorted face, peering to get the sign from the multiple vibrating catchers, dissolved into a howling snowstorm.

"Terrible static!" David backed away, eyeing the rabbit-ears antenna on top of the TV set, and the pitcher reappeared ghost-like through the snow and disappeared again as David reached toward the antenna.

"Have I been electrified?" Like that glass rod experiment – rubbed with silk? Is it me, or…?" David ran out of the living room to look for his portable radio.

The umpire shouted: "Strike two!"

Scowling, the batter bent for a handful of dirt, but no one was watching him in the living room.

David was out on the lawn, twisting the little portable radio from side to side. He ran back into the bedroom.

"Listen, listen, Ted, the static's louder when I turn my portable this way. The aerial's wrapped around a little card inside my portable radio so that it's directional—"

"I don't care about your lousy radio. I don't care about the World Series. All I care about is me. I'm a spotted freak. At least you're purple all over. It's all your fault I am purple-spotted."

"What can I say?" David stared out the window, slowly turning the portable radio toward the sea, and the static blared.

David peered at his brother's swollen purple eyes. "Somebody is shooting at us. We are not giving off static. I think we're reflecting it. Somebody is following each of us with a narrow radio beam — aimed like a fire hose —no, like a laser. We're a couple of targets. That's what I think."

"I don't care about goofy scientific stuff," Ted bleated. "So shut up with all that stuff. It's your fault, you and that lousy reef. I wish I was dead!"

"Don't talk like that. Get my big speargun over there." David carried the portable radio. "Yes, outside. I want you to come outside. All right, put on your hat if you don't want anybody to see your stupid purple head."

David led the way toward the Chalk Cliff.

Ted tagged after him, lugging the heavy speargun. A homemade arbalest powered by four thick strands of rubber surgical tubing, the speargun had driven its steel harpoon shaft clear through a small leopard shark. Above the surface, freed from the resistance of the water, the speargun was more powerful and deadly.

"I'm going to shoot that thing." Ted's purple eyelids slitted, and he glanced about. But there were no amused or pitying faces of neighbors to see his purple-blotched face.

He stopped. Fitting the three-foot long steel shaft into the steel cup, hissing with effort, he stretched the rubber tubing, cocking the spear gun like a hair-trigger crossbow. He ran after his brother.

Ahead, gulls on the updraft white-flagged to the edge of the cliff. David was peering down. His back was bent. He wasn't saying anything.

Ted stumbled. "Look, David, down there! Something shining on top of the water —like a ghost."

"That's what I'm looking at. Sunlight reflecting off the spray, the dried salt, the organs of its body. Hard to see what shape—hey, you little idiot, don't shoot it!"

"Keep away from me, David. You told me to bring the spear gun."

"Don't point it at me! Give it here."

"I'm going to shoot. Keep away."

"Listen, Ted, I told you wrong. Shooting it with the spear gun isn't going to help us. We'll still be purple, Ted. Give me the spear gun. I was a stupid crock to tell you to bring it. Shooting this thing when we don't know what will happen—" David lunged.

Ted scuttled backward along the edge of the cliff.

"Don't you aim it at me, Ted. I told you I was wrong to bring it. Shooting won't solve anything. Look what happened when I stuck a screwdriver in it. I'm just a crock, always poking things with pins or thermometers to see what they will do. Don't shoot it with a spear gun!"

"You keep away from me!"

"Don't shoot it." David's voice softened. "Behind me, you hear the portable radio, hear the static. That stupid thing down there's no worm. Only stupid crocs and gremmies," David's voice rose, "go around sticking and poking and pestering things they don't know anything about!"

"You hear the radio static!" David's voice brightened with a promise. "That thing down there in the surf is broadcasting static, on an authorized wave links. Yes, listen! I know how to make people believe us about this thing— make people take us seriously— so hand me the speargun."

But Ted backed off, his narrow eyes slitted.

"Hand me the speargun." David followed.

"The F.C.C., the Federal Communication's men, remember how they caught me when I broadcast on unauthorized wave links? All we have to do is report this thing, and their tracer equipment will—"

Whirling at the brink of the cliff, Ted fired the speargun. The long steel harpoon shaft flashed downward like an arrow. Ted scrambled down the cliff toward the lashing sea. He wallowed in the purple staining shallows, even ducking his head into the spreading purple dye.

"You stupid little gremmie!" David violently dragged his brother out onto the purple sand. "What did you do that for? Now we don't know what it'll do. After all I said, why, why did you have to go and shoot it?"

"At least," Ted gasped, purple dye streaming down his face, "at least now I am purple all over like you. Leggo!"

But David arm-locked his brother, brushing him toward the cliff. "Butt out of here! That thing is spouting purple like a geyser."

"Hope it dies," Ted wheezed as he climbed the cliff. "Look at my hands, like your hands now. But I don't want purple hands!" He cried out, clawing the purple chalk.

He was sobbing as David shoved him up to the top of the purple-sprayed cliff. Above him, purple gulls and purple fog rose in the updraft and swept inland on the sea wind. As the two boys ran toward home there was a purple mist before their eyes.

P urple faces yelled in horror at each other and scattered into purple houses. A purple policeman stared helplessly at the purple sky.

Purple defense officials shouted into purple telephones. A purple military mind instinctively pushed a purple button. The locks clicked in the deep missile silos. The clocks ticked while an A.S.W. plane, with a long magnetic-anomaly detector protruding from its tail like a stinger, droned low along the cliffs and over the purple surf. Its bomb-bay door opened. A fat gleam of metal tumbled downward through the air and splashed as the plane veered away in frantic evasive action. The purple explosion mushroomed toward the stratosphere.

The organic probe of the third planet had blossomed, seeded.

Catalytic molecules spread with the winds, triggering a film of moisture which coated plants, planarian worms, plagiarists and platypuses, and everything was turning purple.

Purple people ran randomly through the streets of Salt Lake City, Kansas City, Jersey City, their eyeballs purple with outrage.

Purple cows chopped contentedly on the purple grass of Western Europe — and Eastern Europe.

Purple presidents and dictators shouted angrily back and forth via purple-moistured microphones. Louder and louder the static engulfed them. Static on all wavelengths echoed from everyone all over the purple planet.

Even from outer space the earth appeared purple. In perigee beyond the Moon, the translucently organic ship tipped as six eyes peered out, four ears wiggled. Three eyelids fluttered.

"MMMM! What a confusion of broadcasts! Really, you've goofed again. Even both of us can't follow the thought patterns of all four billion of them at once."

"O K K K! O K K K! But mistakes are how we learn. I remember it took you three organic attempts just to dissolve their simple mechanical intruder."

"Really, I should have succeeded but for minor technical difficulties, and bureaucratic interference, insufficient funds—"

"Insufficient brains! My second space spore already is drifting down with a much-improved genetic pattern, more powerful catalyst, twice as radio-reflective, twice as purple!"

"Really, don't you think turning them all so purple, all the same color, will deflect their natural behavior, alter the very habits we've light-yeared so far to study?"

"No!"

"But your radio-reflective tracer diminishes their visible differences. Will it deplete their very exciting savagery?"

"At this stage of the metamorphosis," three eyes narrowed confidently, "I hardly think so!"

The mouth-split smiled. "But it's always fun to experiment!"

THE BUTCHER

Written in St. Augustine FL, in 1951
Setting: An Archaeology Dig in the Southwest

The reason I chose groveling before potsherds as my life work—besides low pay and long hours—was supposed freedom of inquiry. I thought shoveling dirt through a sifting screen would have no destructive consequences.

A sour joke. Now, within wire and guards, they have other archaeologists digging and not telling what they dig. The "Boneyard Project," offering clues with tremendous prehistoric implications, has been shrouded now in the secrecy of "practical military development."

Our original discovery group had a fleeting chance, but stalled and hesitated until we were literally dragged away with clues left dangling. Archaeologists are so used to having all the time in the world. Artifacts don't run away. Harvey, unfortunately, was the one to stumble on the first clue.

Joe blames Harvey, and Harvey, with some justification, blames Joe. Their non-matching personalities caused the stall, all right. We missed out on the biggest who-dunnit since the beginning of life.

If only Harvey had not been a practical joker…. but you find one of those fiends on nearly every student-faculty summer dig. He would drink your beer too.

In our annual hunt for Folsom Man, I was trenching through late Pleistocene gravel, wondering where Harvey disappeared to, when my shovel jammed under what I presumed was a boulder. I applied a few obscenities to Harvey's ancestry, for he should have been helping me.

I levered away, until the tip of my shovel sprung out a vertical strip of rusty iron. Blinking sand out of my eyes, I bent to throw it out of the trench.

I unhesitatingly classified the iron as a somewhat flattened crowbar, probably hammered into formation for some obscure reason by a semi-mythical Irishman building a long mound to the coal deposits at the foot of the Mesa, attempting to construct a permanent and profitable railroad. I casually dated the relic Late Nineteenth Century, A.D.

But as I thought wistfully of the great beer wagons that trundled around in those days, I noticed—where rust had flaked away—little squiggles and curlicues incised in the iron. They resembled runes—pre-Christian Norse writing.

It reminded me of the probably spurious relics and grave markers found in Minnesota lake country, put forth by archaeological dreamers as evidence of post-Vinland Viking penetration.

Although I try to view all discoveries with a jaundiced eye, as I stared, the crowbar assumed the proportions of a two-handled sword blade. I imagined a journal article titled: Graduate Student Makes Notable Discovery.

Of course they would conclude that the sword reached the Raton area by intertribal trade routes, rather than swinging on the hip of a lusty Viking, but no matter. Could it be dated? I regretted having removed it from the gravel. Still, a nice red shell of oxidation would be there.

But it wasn't. The sword was a plant, a phony.

As I stood up waving my disappointment in my hand, Harvey's high laugh came with the wind. That archaeological sadist was watching me through binoculars over the edge of a dry wash.

Even mother nature conspired against me, for Harvey has the physique and cross-country ability of a giraffe.

Naturally when he appeared at noon chow with a breathless story of a propeller embedded in late Pleistocene, we flipped pinto beans at him with our spoons. We were on round ninety-nine of the old mystery of why the Native American horse, the White Horned Bison and other contemporaries of Folsom man became extinct. It was prairie country then, as now. Surely country that could support vast herds of pronghorn, and more recently, bison, could keep a few horses alive. If a tsetse-type fly was the villain, wouldn't there be some variant horses, some hereditary immunity? The black death and the yellow fever never caused the extinction of an entire continent of men. And where are the flies today, or fossil evidence of them, or of diseased horses?

Discussing that conundrum, I said, "Then we have our friend Folsom Man."

"Hardly." Joe laughed. His brown and grey beard was splotched with gobs from dinner, but we dared not laugh, for he was Chairman of the Department. "Even a dense population in an agrarian culture, armed only with crude spear-throwers, could not hunt down all our brave horses."

"But Professor," said Dr. Leiss, a nervous bridge player and the world's most non-understandable lecturer, "dese little equus vouldn't haf to all die. Ven a cerdan reduction iss reached, species survival margin iss gone and the vurst beeg vinter iss beginning of de end. Sometime ven udder vactors are tough, the Folsom spear breaks the back of a species."

Joe wasn't listening. "Harvey, why are you staring at me?"

"Sir, I've been trying to speak to you off and on for ten minutes, but you didn't seem to hear me. I'm worried the altitude is giving you eardrum trouble again."

Joe slapped his ear as if trying to knock water out of its mate.

"What about?"

"This propeller, sir." He had run back and exhumed it.

"That is no propeller. It's from a turbine, and worn out at that. Undoubtedly a government experimental jet crashed in this area."

That might have been the end of it. But a company of bone hunters usually includes a hunter of the Grail, a poor man's geologist with a click box, earphones, and government poster offering $10,000 bounty for anything resembling solid uranium. Our bounty hunter was named Albert.

He must have had a Geiger counter in his head, because he got up and went in the tent where his equipment reposed. He casually stuck out his head and announced, "That propeller is radioactive as all hell."

When we reapproached the camp, Albert was waving the counter over the propellor and grinning, a grin that faded the closer we approached. But Joe seemed more interested in the prop than the demise of Albert.

"Did I hold it too long?" Harvey gaped at Albert.

"Heck no, it's not that radioactive. I meant it's damned radioactive compared with the background count."

"Amazing, so the Air Force has already tested an atomic powered plane and it crashed near here." Joe has a gluttony common to many scientists. Since he holds nuclear physics to be merely a subdivision of archeology, he gobbles it with complete confidence. He'd be happy to advise Oppenheimer on any little problem.

"Undoubtedly this pile heats the air, also drawing it in by convection when the ship is traveling too slowly to operate as a ramjet. A heat-power converter, no doubt a mercury vapor turbine, drives the main air compressor turbine. This so-called propellor is one of the rotating multiple blades. Harvey, where did you find it?"

"Sir, if it's secret stuff, maybe we'd better keep our noses out. There are enough investigations going on in universities now. With only one semester to go, I don't want to be flunked as a spy."

"Nonsense, Harvey, but only you and I will go. The other three gentlemen will find Folsom Man more enlightening."

"Vot are you inferring, Professor," Dr. Leiss almost screamed. "Already I haf been cleared sefen times!"

Harvey and Joe returned soon but separately. They were not speaking to each other.

"What happened?" I whispered to Harvey.

"He found a piece of copper washstand pipe sticking out of the side of the dry wash. He thinks it's another joke."

"What was he expecting to find?"

"How the devil should I know?"

"There were never any houses out here. He knew you planted it. I'll bet the old boy is consulting his conscience, as to whether to expel you now or wait till the end of the semester and give you a smiling F."

"Listen, just because I have a good sense of humor is no reason for you mossbacks to make me a whipping boy." He left me standing there as he walked away stiff-legged and angry.

Albert had to hop a plane back to the university for an ultra-heavy date or something. Since Harvey was over in the sagebrush talking to himself, Albert put the propeller in his laundry sack. "When he recognizes you again, tell him this is such a peculiar looking alloy I'm going to show it to a buddy of mine in metallurgy and let him guess."

The next morning, to arrest the growth of Harvey's persecution complex, I let him take me up to where he found the propeller.

The copper pipe had green-stained the area for several inches around. I was just going to complement Harvey on the neatest job of planting I had ever seen, but I noticed a knob of metal the same dull silvery color as the prop.

Suspiciously I began to dig, and dig, and dig. The knob became a rod extending back into the bank about the length of my arm, where it met the end of a large cylinder with a three-inch wall of the same alloy.

This was too much work to be a plant. I thought maybe the Atomic Energy Commission might have had some installation out here and then covered it up. But that did not deter me from digging.

The cylinder turned out to be sliced lengthwise, a shoot or trough with a diameter of about eight feet. While I dug at that end, Harvey climbed on top of the embankment, walked about ten paces straight away from the wash, then dug down. He struck it.

By this time, I was beginning to puff. I watched him walk another ten yards and put down another hole, ending in the clink of metal on metal. He went twenty yards farther and did it again. I scrambled up and ran about hundred yards, in line with his holes, and struck it. Harvey leapfrogged another hundred beyond me and finally didn't strike it. Either it curved or we didn't feel like any more digging without a drink of water.

"You notice how the inside has hard encrustations on it, like limestone growths on the walls of Carlsbad? Do you think it would take more than heat and oxidation to do that?"

"I got a D in Chem 1-A," I replied.

When we couldn't ignore Joe's shout any longer, we went back down the wash and shoveled dirt onto sifting screens until nightfall without telling him what we had found. Harvey spoke only when spoken to, and I was waiting for Harvey to speak. My mistake. Joe is Mr. Keene with a shovel and a pick. His two and two might have come very close to four.

Dawn found Harvey and I poking around the enigma. At first, the main thing that bothered us was how AEC, or whoever buried that longitudinal slice of pipe, had laid it in late Pleistocene without disturbing the more recent sedimentary layers. Had it been driven in through the vertical bank of the wash? There were no signs that heavy equipment necessary for such an understandable operation had ever been mounted in the wash, no post-holes, no grease spots, no tire tracks. But there were a few oddly machined lumps of metal. Digging deeper into the bank, I found more.

Also I was intrigued, as I had been the day before, by a dense layer of bones. For the most part they were ribs from horses and bison. If more or less complete skeletons had been present, I'd have said the animal herds had been suddenly overcome by ash from a volcanic eruption; many of the bones were slightly charred. But there was not a skull in the lot.

Harvey, who had been working on top of the prairie with a post hole digger, yelled that he found a chunk of metal in conjunction with more bones. And it seemed to me, standing in the wash, that the bottom layer of bones corresponded with the bottom of the long metal shoot or trough, or whatever it was. The whole business gave me a headache.

If I had not belonged to the cautious school of scientists, I would have been tempted to date these evidences of advanced technology as fifteen or twenty thousand B.C. The American Pleistocene, as defined by characteristic fauna, extended until then. Thus, the metal would be contemporary with Folsom Man. Although we flaked out some beautiful javelin points, this wandering hunter had not left any evidence of blast furnaces or foundries, or of aptitude in that direction.

If we had been in Egypt instead of New Mexico, I would have been tremendously excited. Since I'm not an Egyptologist, I would've been able to delude myself that here was evidence of a lost art of alloy metalwork dating from the supposed dawn of the Neolithic age, or earlier!

"Hey," Harvey yelled in my ear, "Snap out of it. Look what I uprooted."

He poked me in the stomach with a pitted, worn-out looking rod, black with carbon deposit, projecting from a glass–insulated, shiny cylinder. It was about the size of a World War II gas mask container. From the back, extending under his armpit, a green-corroded tube angled nearly to the ground. The end of it was threaded.

The glass insulator, or whatever it was, was not even chipped.

"Hit it with your mineralogy hammer," said Harvey.

"Heck no."

"OK, I'll show you where I banged it with a shovel when I was digging it up."

He placed his finger on a dent in the glass and said, "Plastic."

I held my cigarette lighter under it. It was a quick heat conductor, and when I wiped it off, I saw the flame had no more effect than if it had been glass.

"They're doing wonders with synthetic resins these days." Harvey laughed in a higher voice than usual.

Since there is no such thing as malleable silica at 87°, I had to nod my head affirmatively.

The thing had several corroded knobs protruding through the plastic. Harvey and I hammered and twisted these, on the chance they would release one of the end pieces and let us see inside. But they broke off.

"You know," Harvey suggested, "we could be making a mistake, fooling around with this thing. It could be radioactive. Or it could be some sort of loaded gun."

"Or an electric welding device, or a beer can opener," I replied. "It's out of balance for a gun, and there's no good way to hold onto it unless something has come unscrewed from that end."

I edged away, not expressing my fear that it might be something tested in an atomic explosion and dumped out here as too hot to play around with. I began to develop psychosomatic symptoms of radioactive poisoning.

Without a word between us, we headed back to camp for soap and water and for the click box. While we were scrubbing our hands, Joe caught us and ordered us to the shovels and sifting screens.

It was late afternoon before we could get back to the mystery. The perhaps-gun did not accelerate the clicks, but the big chute did. The Geiger buzzed like a rattlesnake. Whether this meant it was hot enough to be dangerous, we didn't know. But we stayed well away as we dug into the jackstraw piles of bones. Pieces of machine metal the size of hen's eggs were mixed with bones. The metal pieces were irregular in shape, as if created for varied and incomprehensible purposes. Those did not excite the Geiger counter.

I suggested we quit burrowing around like school boys. By ourselves, we weren't going to be able to find the score. The one thing we could do, before running to Joe, was get some idea of the extent of the bone bed.

We walked a thousand yards along the direction the chute pointed, putting down post holes every so often and striking bone every time. In some places, the bones were predominantly horse ribs. In other places, there were mostly leg bones and shoulder blades—from a few bison but mostly horse. Even when we worked another thousand yards south, at right angles to our first line of holes, we did not find any skulls. Some bones were charred, some not.

As we dug back toward the wash, we struck an area of vertebrae. Harvey is usually a volcano of impossible theories. But he was as quiet as I was, when we squatted by the gun-looking thing again. Whatever it was seemed to have burned out and been thrown away.

The sun crept down behind sagebrush.

"We sampled a square of about a million square yards," I said. "I estimate each square yard contains parts of three animals. However, each animal is divided into three sections, which means about an animal per square yard. Skull piles may take up some of that area, although we didn't strike any, so I scale the total number of animals down to around eight thousand within our sample."

"I'm going home," said Harvey.

"They were killed fifteen or twenty thousand years ago."

"It's getting dark." Harvey shoved the gun into an excavation. I left it there but pocketed one of the oddly shaped pieces of metal.

For once I was glad to see Joe's goaty face across the campfire.

When I handed him the metal, he sneered. "So, you whip out abstract sculpture instead of Folsom Man artifacts. What does this represent? Or am I supposed to caress it with my hands and eyes and never ask, for it is art so pure, so far above the level that… Harvey, why are you staring at me?"

"You better tell him," Harvey said, mindful of his own ill repute.

Very slowly and conservatively, I did. I took my time. Harvey and I had already wasted a couple of days. Archaeologists have no contempt for time, except for huge chunks of it.

Joe kept watching, waiting for Harvey to laugh, but I have a reputation for careful investigation, and I am not given to pranks. Gradually, Joe began to lean forward and forget about Harvey. He scraped the piece of metal with his pocket knife as though expecting to find a Made-in-Japan label. He tossed it to Dr. Leiss.

"Undoubtedly that is some sort of turbine fitting. An immense atomic-powered plane exploded in the air, but at a low altitude. It must have driven a section of turbine into the bank where a herd of American horse had been overcome by volcanic disturbance some fifteen million years before."

Patiently, I repeated my objective observations, this time adding a few interpretations. There were no signs of a recent explosion in the area. The chute or trough did not look at all like part of a turbine. It looked more like something a rocket might have been launched from. The encrustations inside it could have been caused by rocket exhaust. Unbroken strata extended right to the edges of it. There was no sign it had been driven in after the strata were laid down. It looked to me as if it had been on the surface about the time the bones were.

"Furthermore," I said, "it was in the middle of a systematic slaughtering ground."

But Joe was staring at Harvey, who was scraping chili con carne off a tin plate.

"Do you have to be so noisy while I'm listening?"

"That's a helicopter," Harvey replied.

It was. After landing, three husky men emerged with badges pinned on their wallets, with one underfed apologetic man with a too-long overcoat, obviously a scientist. He thanked us for having such a bright campfire, handed Harvey a flashlight, and said, "Take us where Albert Kendall said you dug."

While Harvey led long-overcoat and one husky up the wash, a second husky showed off his shorthand as we answered how old we were, the last time we planned to overthrow the government by violence, and that sort of thing. The third husky sat in the helicopter, talking into a microphone.

When Harvey and the other two came back, the huskies explained penalties for giving out "classified information." Every bird we saw, every Folsom point we found, was classified. Until scientists intervened, the huskies weren't going to let us take back any Folsom artifacts. Dr. Leiss, they stared at, until the man was on the verge of tears.

That was the end of the summer dig.

Joe told me, after I was cleared this past autumn, the area had been blocked off by the military, and a couple of diffusionists from the State Archaeology Department were directing excavations. Naturally he is so jealous that his current set of lectures has degenerated into diatribes against the government.

Albert told me when he showed the propeller to his pal, that egg had run to his metallurgy prof with it… and soon found a guy with a badge tapping him on the shoulder.

Dr. Leiss is now spooning yogurt for his duodenal ulcer.

Harvey, loudly bitter, is doing annual maneuvers with the National Guard, which makes a case of beer last a lot longer than in this rock garden. Beer, you know, adds a special luster to flint.

As a newsboy's urgent shouts rise from the street, I am quietly polishing Folsom points. I wonder in whose century the butcher will pay Earth another visit.

ARCTIC INVASION

Formerly under the title, The Eskimo Invasion,
nominated for 1966 Nebula Award: Best Novelette
and the 1967 Hugo Award: Best Novelette.
This story was later incorporated into Hayden's
Nebula-nominated novel, The Eskimo Invasion.
Note: it wasn't until 1977 the word Eskimo
was replaced by the word Inuit.

I

Snow stalked him like a spectral white bear. Through his arctic sunglasses, Dr. Joe West squinted. His forehead ached from the penetrating white glare.

Across the dazzling ice, shadow-shapes of children and squatty men romped on all fours. They were pretending to be bears, roaring and giggling as the bears devoured the children. Watching from their summer parkas with hoods turned back, the horde of swollen women exposed their squinting babies to the Arctic sun.

It had been three days since the event, the birth.

For two days since Dr. West concluded these people could *not* be Eskimos, he had been trying to leave. Escape still seemed too strong a word to use.

"Today we go," Dr. West said, or… asked.

"Soon-soon we go," Edwardluk agreed pleasantly; his was the only dog team in the encampment, only seven dogs for over a hundred Eskimos. "Soon as this person's leg is better."

"Your leg *is* better. Last sleep." Dr. West squinted down at his stethoscope, which dangled from Edwardluk's thick neck. "I gave you my heart ears, and you said your leg felt better. You said we would go today."

"Eh-eh," Edwardluk laughed, politely agreeing with whatever the whiteman was saying, "leg is better than yesterday. Eh-eh, you are better. Each day you like us better. Tomorrow, you like this person better still."

"I like you now," Dr. West tried to restrain the irritation in his voice. "As soon as we travel to the whitemen, I'll tell them how much you helped me. As I've been telling you, the airplanes will drop much food for this camp. We must go!"

"Eh-eh," Edwardluk suddenly seemed to agree with enthusiasm. "Soon as we kill seals to feed dogs, we go!"

Edwardluk trotted toward his tent, and Dr. West followed with long strides, unable to believe this sudden activity.

"First we fill our bellies." Edwardluk flopped down on an ancient seal skin and shouted impressively for his wife to cut meat. There was little, although The Canadian Cultural Sanctuary Commission had restocked the Boothia district with twin-birth seals. "Then we sleep."

"But now is our chance to hunt seals," Dr. West protested, pointing with his recoilless rifle toward the shore ice where a crack had opened, where seals could rise.

"Hunt seals," Edwardluk agreed like an echo. He added helpfully: "Good dream protects us from bad ice. Good dream help you like us better tomorrow." With downcast eyes, Edwardluk smiled like a shy little boy and handed Dr. West a thawing glob of seal liver as if it were a Valentine. "Best piece for you."

Edwardluk's smiling eyes narrowed as his massive jaw crunched through the partially frozen meat. Gulping, he swallowed and crunched and gulped. His eyes closed with pure joy. His head sagged down. As easily as a tired child, he slept.

Dr. West's strong young hands tightened on his recoilless rifle. *These people are so obliging, so innocent, so damned lovable, it would be impossible to shoot. Damn! Damn, damn, damn!*

If I'm a prisoner, he thought, I could escape. I *can escape whenever I choose to use – threaten to use—force.*

Dr. West's contradictory grin, which also made him attractive to women who were more selective than Eskimo women, cracked his chapped lips. *If I am a prisoner*, his thoughts echoed, *I can escape. If I am not a prisoner, by definition I cannot escape.*

Damn! That's a neurotic thought. I've got to escape.

He stared down at the scrap of meat attracting flies to Edwardluk's small hand. These unusual people lacked the gargantuan appetites of Eskimos. Also contrary to Eskimos, there were too many small children. More than the environment could support. The disproportionate number of children indicated a rapid increase in population. After 36 days with these people, Dr. West had written down too many observations. What he observed three nights ago was the absolute end.

If I don't leave now, I may never leave. Grinning, grimacing, he shook his head. *Damn! Got to escape.*

He glanced from the snoring Edwardluk to the sleeping dogs. Yesterday when he tried to order these people to help him prepare a sled, giggling they had diverted him from leaving. Marthalik had rubbed urgently against him, peeping up with sweet narrow eyes, urging him to come back into the tent, ducking under his waving arms of anger. He felt trapped.

In her hood the wrinkled face of the baby flopped back-and-forth and began to cry. From Dr. West's inexplicable rage, the people had averted their faces like hurt children. His determination to use force, to seize a sled and a prisoner, dissolved in embarrassment, remorse, a dark tent and gentle whispering with Marthalik yesterday. Today.

In the white glare his eyelids itched. Dr. West knew if he was going to travel, he should already have left. *These women, these incredibly wonderful women. I've got to escape now!* Simultaneously, he felt like laughing and crying.

Beyond the shore-ice and the dark crack, gleamed the veined sea-ice with distant islands glittering, icebergs. *God help me! I have to cross that!* He knew the Canadian Cultural Sanctuary Guardpost must be somewhere beyond that glowing horizon.

Five years ago, during his Alaskan Eskimo population survey, Dr. West had learned how difficult it was for a Kabloona, a whiteman, to handle Eskimo dogs, but he had done it. *I can do it now if the dogs are harnessed to the sled.*

Flies buzzed above Edwardluk's sleeping smile, and his massive jaw moved. He was dreaming. These people, Marthalik, all of them, had such animated faces when they slept, as if their dreams were reality.

But reality to Dr. West was burning eyelids and the shock of the thirty-third night. *Got to escape. Must outsmart Edwardluk.*

Quietly, Dr. West rolled up his sleeping bag. He slid his arm through the sling of his recoilless rifle, the only rifle in the encampment since the disappearance of Edwardluk's "brother," who had owned a rusty rifle and had rusty personality to match and seemed more like a real Eskimo.

That brother had been troubled by lice. But these people had no lice. These people had no tuberculosis. They were *not* the Eskimos of the Canadian Arctic.

Dr. West hefted his pack. Heavy-laden, he started the long walk across the ice toward the distant icebergs in the polar gulf. He hoped he was setting a trap for Edwardluk.

Dr. West's original intention had been to take one of these remarkable people back with him. There was still that possibility…

With each step, the silicone rubber membrane in Dr. West's boots exhaled fog. Yet he waded with dry feet through shimmering puddles of melt-water across the thawing sea-ice. Like a giant, he strode over eroding streambeds on the ice. Freshwater trickled toward dark leads where the sea surged, where seals could rise.

This summer ice was rotting, dangerous. He opened the vents in his outer parka because to perspire was also dangerous. "Bad, bad-bad," Edwardluk had said, "for whiteman to walk alone on sea-ice."

Then you come rescue me, Dr. West thought, and walked on and on.

The icebergs seemed no closer, but when Dr. West looked back, he saw that the encampment had miniaturized into a cluster of dots.

Like a midget, a midge, a dark spec, Dr. West plotted endlessly across the flat sea-ice. He hoped Edwardluk was watching, massive jaw beginning to sag with worry.

Dr. West was gambling, possibly his life, that Edwardluk would grunt with decision, hitch the dogs to the sled and come out from that cluster of specs.

"Biggest 'skimo camp ever!" the nervous bush pilot had marveled when he set Dr. West down on the ice thirty-six days ago. "Where'd they all come from? Out you go, Dr. No-Name. Can't risk my license, even for all those plump little reasons waving to me out there. Got to take off." The expatriate Englishman's gaze swept the vast arctic sky. "Cultural Sanctuary's patrol aircraft's likely airborne now, and hot after our vanished radar blip. Serious charges, landing on the Boothia Peninsula. Got to takeoff. Me aircraft's me life!"

The self-taught pilot, an ex-R.A.F. ground crewman, had not reappeared in two weeks as promised, or in three weeks, or in four weeks. Crashed, Dr. West suspected. If radar-tracked and arrested, the pilot would have blabbed by now, and a Cultural Sanctuary patrol plane would have swooped low, searching for Dr. West.

Dr. West's application for a landing permit had been denied by the Cultural Sanctuary Commission in Ottawa. Not even Overflight Permits were being granted anywhere near the North Magnetic Pole. Dr. West suspected that politics or professional jealousy was behind the refusal. Perhaps the ethnological bigwigs at McGill University wanted first to look at the rumored population increase but hadn't gotten around to it yet. Surely, they didn't think Dr. Joseph West—a former director researching population problems at the University of California but now unemployed— had become a smuggler of transistor radios and steel tools which could culturally dislocate the Boothia Eskimos. There was a little evidence of recent cultural smuggling to these people.

Dr. West shook his head. If what he had observed continued, these people were more apt to dislocate the world than vice versa.

His pack-straps sawed into his shoulders. His feet plodded on and on across the sea-ice. He squinted at the sky, although he had given up all hope of being arrested, rescued by a Cultural Sanctuary aircraft. The only way of carrying his warning message to the Outside seemed to be through hopeful physical exertion, plus guile if Edwardluk fell into his trap.

Above the peak of the iceberg, a flock of dark fulmars whirled. Around the berg gleamed broken ice and dark water where sea birds could feed. Dr. West was surprised that he did not sight a single seal as he circled behind the berg.

Now he was out of view from the camp. Dr. West hoped Edwardluk was harnessing the dogs. *If his friendship talk was genuine, he'll come to rescue me. If not, he'll come to recapture me.* But there was a third possibility, unfortunately. Edwardluk might simply go to sleep – because he couldn't give a damn.

From his pack, Dr. West took out a pad of caribou skin and sat down. Rifle propped against his thigh, he waited. The trap was set for Edwardluk. And waited.

Cold rose through the ancient caribou skin pad into Joe West's haunches. Restlessly, he remembered his Alaskan Eskimos had used bearskin pads because they were thicker. But these Boothia people owned no polar bear skins. They said they never killed their father-bear, and Dr. West was inclined to believe them. The cold enfolded him. From the corner of his eye, a small part of the white background trotted across his field of vision. It was an arctic fox, plume-tailed and oblivious.

Suddenly the white fox stared at him, then passed him. Dr. West felt a creeping urge to look behind his own back. He remembered that the Eskimos refer to the white fox as the bear's dog. On sea-ice, the fox follows the polar bear, dependent on the bear's kills. The Eskimos say: "Fox on ice, look behind you quick, is bear."

Turning his head, Dr. West squinted at each white mound and fuzzy shadow. At point-blank range, he knew a polar bear would appear more cream-colored than the ice. A black spot would be the nose of the polar bear. The Eskimos say: "Bear hold white paw over nose, bear gone, eh-eh. Bear still there."

"Ha!" Dr. West shouted, standing up. The immense white background remained immobile. From the white mounds, a polar bear's head did not rise weasel-like on its long neck.

"Spooked myself. These people talk too much about bears." Dr. West twisted his chilled face into another grin. He didn't want to remember Edwardluk's wide-eyed face above the seal oil lamp.

L ike Eskimos, these people entertained themselves with night stories. Edwardluk's thick neck tilting from side to side, eyes closing in ecstasy, he had grunted like a bear. "Grandfather of the sky!" Edwardluk's suddenly hoarse voice creaked. "Sharpen your hunger. We – your children – prepare for you. Open your jaws!"

Dr. West blinked his eyes and shivered. If their grandfather was a bear spirit, that was all right with Dr. West. Who was he to deride anyone's totems or religious beliefs? But after 36 days, what grated on his nerves was the continuously nonanthropomorphic theology of their night stories. These people had things backward, he thought.

The mythology of other Eskimos, real Eskimos, presented bear spirits as merely helping or hindering men. Man was the end-purpose.

But in these people's stories, the bear seemed the end-purpose. The people helped the bear. The people prepared the seals, the rocks, and the airplanes for the bear. This was not the bear on the ice. This was a bear in the sky. The purpose of all life seems to funnel into the bear.

What their bear symbolized, Dr. West had not found out, but he had had enough experience with real bears to suspect that a hungry polar bear makes little distinction between a prone man and a seal. He remained standing, clutching his rifle. The non-appearance of seals in the open water around this iceberg suggested a real bear was nearby.

Dr. West's eyes watered with the strain of trying to see everything and distinguishing less and less in the white glow of the ice. The cold soaked up through his feet. His leg bones became conductors of the cold. Sometimes he stood motionless, forgetting to stamp his feet. His vision and sense of time blurred.

The fulmars cried out an alarm, whirling dark wings upward into the sky. Dr. West's eyes widened. He turned, then laughed with relief. A line of black specks across the ice became dogs pulling a distant sled.

Dr. West sat down on his caribou skin pad, but his heart was thudding with suppressed excitement, and he stood up. Peering, suddenly he cursed.

There was more than one man approaching. A man trotted ahead of the sled. The dark bulge on the sled was a second man, probably Edwardluk. Far behind, a third man plodded over the ice.

Three men were more than Dr. West had bargained for, even though he had the only gun.

By the time they were close, Dr. West still had not decided what to do.

"He was watching you!" Edwardluk shouted happily. "Up there he was watching you."

Dr. West stared up at the peak of the iceberg. If Edwardluk was referring to an actual bear, it was invisible to Dr. West. He squinted at the dogs, who lay down; they had not scented a bear.

"Seen us coming." Edwardluk made a circling motion with his wide face and stubby nose. Dr. West supposed the bear had circled out of sight behind the berg.

"We come to carry back your seals," Edwardluk said innocently.

The second man stood smiling at the sky. The third man still was approaching. They seemed unarmed. In their fur parkas they reminded Dr. West of three childhood teddy bears. They had been kind and hospitable to Dr. West, and now he couldn't quite bring himself to point the rifle. He didn't want to threaten them with harsh words which would bring hurt expressions to their childlike faces. He didn't want to kidnap a prisoner.

Swiftly he rationalized that it might be dangerous to take a prisoner who might chew through his bonds while Dr. West slept. *Let some anonymous expedition seize the first laboratory specimen.*

"There's a dead seal under the edge of the ice," Dr. West blurted, pointing with his rifle barrel and walking behind their backs to the sled. Their harpoons still were lashed to the sled.

"Eh-eh," Edwardluk's voice agreed politely to the lie. "There is a seal, but my eyes don't see it yet."

Dr. West's shivering hands were tying his pack and sleeping bag on the sled.

"Ha!" Dr. West shouted at the dogs as he flopped on the sled, and to his surprise and relief the dogs lurched forward before he could use the whip. They dashed past the startled face of the third man. Back to camp was where the dogs were hurrying. Slashing the whip with all his strength, Dr. West managed to turn the leader toward the ice horizon.

T he sled passed in an arc through the shouting range of the running men, but Dr. West managed to whip the dogs away, the sled weaving a snake-like course beyond the iceberg with Edwardluk running far behind.

I have escaped, Dr. West thought inaccurately.

The terrible global significance of what he had observed about these people he had not fully analyzed. Mainly he was fleeing from what happened on the 33rd night, and from his contradictory desire to go back to them. To the women –

He clung to the sled undulating over the ice. The wonder of the 33rd night. The dogs were running uncontrollably.

The shock of the 33rd night. The sled bounced over a pressure ridge. The women –

If he let go, he would fall off the sled and go back. He laughed with bewilderment. It was these women who would be too much for the world.

Dr. West had been with many women as he made his way through college, Med school, hospitals, traveling from Cambridge Mass to Berkely California, then—researching population and genetics—on expeditions to the Alaskan Tundra, Moosejaw Saskatchewan, the Coppermine Northwest Territories, and now the Boothia Peninsula.

These remarkable women on the Boothia Peninsula were so much more . . . *I'm crazy to be leaving*, he thought.

He clung to the bounding sled, trying to blank out the 33rd night and his incredible first experience with Marthalik.

T he sled runner jammed in broken ice. The sled almost capsized as it abruptly stopped. His sunglasses slid down his nose. Blinking, Dr. West slid off the sled, hoisted the rudder free and shouted at the dogs, who surged forward. Dr. West found himself loping behind the sled, trying to overtake it, running. He fell, dislodging his glasses as he lunged through the blinding white glare, almost seizing the sled, getting across a puddle of meltwater. Springing up, running hard and shouting angrily at the dogs, he had thought they would stop, but they were veering off to the left. Their loose gate accelerated to an excited rush, as if they had scented a seal.

His commanding shouts grew shrill. Desperately he ran a shorter course to head them off, but they were bounding too fast, the lightened sled skipping behind them. Without the sled he was helpless, hopeless. His eyesight whirled with blinding lights. He tripped.

Kneeling upward, gasping with breathless panic, he unslung his rifle. In the glare, his twitching eye could barely distinguish the front sight as it shook back and forth. Aiming ahead of the dogs he fired.

Unchecked, the dogs ran into the blinding distance. He fired and fired. A dog turned end for end, biting its rump as the other dogs dragged it along. A dog in front of the sled yelped and was mounted by the sled runners as a team swept on. Dragging two writhing dogs and the swerving sled, the dog team charged on like troops into battle.

The leader abruptly stopped as he reached an open lead. The ski sled skidded sideways, braked only by the bodies of the two wounded dogs from sliding into the dark water and engulfing them all.

The dog teams stood looking back at Dr. West, their breath fogging. If there had been a seal, it was long gone.

Kabloona, you panicked. Dr. West blundered toward the team's watching eyes and steaming grins.

His unprotected eyes were shimmering and blurring but he had to recapture the sled before he could go back to search for his dark glasses.

One dog lay limply entangled with the sled. The other whined and sniffed at its shattered spine.

The sled dogs watched, their tongues lolling out of great grins, while he pointed the rifle muzzle at the wounded dog's ear, closed his eyes and pulled the trigger. His hand trembling, Dr. West cut through the leather traces and freed both dogs. Squinting against the whiteness, he tried to see back along the sled runners' trail all the way to the indistinct pressure ridge where he thought he had fallen, where he had lost his glasses.

He was afraid Edwardluk and the other two would have heard the shots, but they should be a long way off near the iceberg. Surely that was a different iceberg. His eyes were killing him!

To reduce the glare, he slit his handkerchief and tied it across his eyes. Almost blinded, he shouted at the dogs, pushed the sled, yelled, cursed, flailed with the whip while dogs dodged in every direction, and suddenly the dog team darted, curved, and flowed along their back-trail toward the pressure ridge. He intended to allow himself one minute to search for his sunglasses.

"Kabloona, here are your snow eyes!" Edwardluk stood, holding the dark glasses above his head.

Dr. West tore off the handkerchief but did not see the other two men in ambush.

"Hand me the glasses." Dr. West did not point the rifle directly at Edwardluk.

Edwardluk's small hand extended the sunglasses. "Bad dogs run away," his voice murmured, and he ducked his head as if ashamed. He shuffled his mukluks on the ice. "This poor person couldn't run fast enough to permit this poor person to—"

"I cannot return to camp," Dr. West interrupted. "I must go find the other whitemen now."

"The other whitemen," Edwardluk agreed like an echo, and his real thinking emerged circuitously. "Bad ice. Two dogs no more. We like you. We help you always. When ice is safe, we go. Tomorrow. Each day you will like us better."

Dr. West became aware of movement behind him, talked fast. "I cannot go back. I'll help you. I'll tell the whitemen your babies are hungry. I'll send food. Because I like you," he insisted rapidly. "I like you. Great bear eat me if I lie."

Edwardluk looked up, and his shy smile widened. "Eh-eh, you want to go, we go! Someday we People help the whitemen. When we are many, help much. Help whitemen of the whole world." Like a tiny giant, Edwardluk spread his arms and left, unaware that the world is 24,000 miles in circumference at the equator, that there are six billion white-whitemen, yellow-whitemen, and black-whitemen, that their vast machines rumble and lurch toward the stars.

"Ha!" Edwardluk shouted at the dogs and cracked the whip. The sled rushed off carrying Dr. West, and Edwardluk, running alongside, shouted: "There is the mountain."

"Which direction is the post?" Dr. West meant the Cultural Sanctuary Guard Post, whose radar the bush pilot had tried to avoid.

"Eh-eh, my brother has been there, and this person's eyes turned inward see. On a line past the mountain, past the island three-four sleeps. The whitemen will see this person helping you."

IV

The dogs soon tired, and Dr. West trotted beside the sled toward the gleaming horizon.

Slipping, tiring, he jammed the muzzle of his rifle into the ice as he fell and rose, muttering, staggering after the relentlessly gliding sled. He was encased in perspiration as he slogged into the blinding sun.

The idea came to him in his exhaustion. If Edwardluk's plan was to wear him out and then seize the rifle . . .

When the sled snagged on a pressure ridge, Dr. West lay on the sled. The dogs lay down.

"Eh-eh!" Edwardluk scampered about with seemingly inexhaustible energy trying to sight a seal, forcing two of the harpoon shafts into the ice, erecting a tattered caribou skin windbreak. "Eh-eh, you rest in camp. This person talk to seal, eh-eh." He hefted the last harpoon. He walked into the distance.

The wind whistled just over the ice, bending the caribou skins into a funnel, a wind-funnel directed at Dr. West's congealing body. Edwardluk had vanished. Shivering, Dr. West ceased to know he was shivering until his ears awoke him to the distant grunting of a polar bear.

"Eh-eh," Edwardluk laughed. "He don't find no seals either."

The dogs whined, but their tone was not hunger. Dr. West's eyelids seemed glued together. The dogs voices whined with fear. Alaskan Eskimo dogs would have been roaring with eagerness to rush along the scent of the polar bear, he thought. These dogs were whining.

Dr. West slid his fingers under his sunglasses to his throbbing eyelids. Overpowering light penetrated, although his eyes were closed. His head ached with pain messages from his overloaded optic nerves. When he tried to open his eyes, he gasped, drowned in dazzling liquid light.

He was snow-blind.

The distant bear emitted a hoarse cough. Dr. West's hand tightened on his rifle. When a bear is hungry enough, he thought, it will stalk sled dogs lying on the ice like seals. When a bear is starving, he sees nothing but seals, and I am blind.

"Eh-eh," Edwardluk's voice laughed, "nothing but seals. Give me the rifle. Big noise will tell bear we are not seals."

"I will hold the rifle," Dr. West replied; he was afraid the rifle was all he had, snow-blind and helpless. "I know how to work it."

"This person knows how to work it," Edwardluk volunteered, and Dr. West could hear him moving closer. "My brother had one and he shot it all the time."

But not at bears, Dr. West thought.

"At bears." Edwardluk's voice persisted. "My brother shot a bear and that is why he vanished. It was bad for him to kill a bear." Prior to this Edwardluk's story had been that his brother had vanished while traveling to get more presents from the whitemen of the big whale-kayak, the whitemen with beautiful red stars on their caps.

"You would not shoot the bear even if I gave you the rifle," Dr. West replied, clinging to the rifle.

"Eh-eh," agreed Edwardluk, "this person is not a bear killer like my brother. This person would only shoot a loud noise so the bear hears we are not seals." He shuffled away.

Dr. West clicked off the safety catch. The recoilless rifle boomed, kicking viciously. There had been ice in the barrel, but it had not burst. "I have frightened the bear." Now there was no need for Edwardluk to have the rifle.

"If this person had the rifle, a seal could be shot." Edwardluk's voice moved closer.

"There are three harpoons," Dr. West replied.

"But your eyes are bad," Edwardluk began circuitously.

"I will not give you the rifle."

Further away the polar bear made a strange mooing noise.

"This person watched while you sleep," Edwardluk said, as if this were more important than the circling bear. "Eh-eh, asleep you frown, you twist. In the encampment it was this way also. You look unhappy when asleep. My brother was that way. Even with arms around woman, your sleep-face is unhappy. Are all whitemen unhappy when they sleep?"

"How the hell should I know?" Dr. West slung his rifle over his back and crawled blindly onto the sled. "Let's go!"

"Whitemen do not shoot the people?" Edwardluk asked. "As if we are dogs?"

"No, I was frightened when I shot the dogs. I thought they were running away. I thought they were leaving me alone to die. I only shoot things that are leaving me to die."

J oe West clung on the dragging sled, his head muffled in the darkness of caribou skin, his eyes throbbing and flashing lights of pain. Once he heard Edwardluk shouting to someone, and his stomach contracted. He dreamed Edwardluk had circled back to the encampment. No escape. Then he realized Edwardluk had merely admonished the dogs.

The sled was moving sporadically as if the dogs were exhausted.

Motionless, Dr. West was awakened by a distant crackle-whoosh of a recoilless rifle. Whitemen? Dr. West's fingers glide along the oddly thin stock of his rifle. He was holding onto a harpoon shaft. "My rifle. He's stolen my rifle."

The dogs whined, hungrily straining, but the sled creaked immovably because Edwardluk had anchored it to the ice so the dogs could not rush forward at the sound of the shot, which meant seal meat. Edwardluk's plodding return and a dragging sound were overwhelmed by the roaring lunges of the dogs. Edwardluk was feeding the dogs first, hurling thuds of meat within their harnessed range. Then he was beating them off. "No more! Got no more!"

"Here is the warm liver." Edwardluk must have carried it under his parka. "Eat. This person left a little blubber by the water for the bear. Eat. The great bear will see how we help the bear. Eat. Soon this person shoots a bigger seal. Then this person will eat."

From the distance rose a long-drawn howling roar like a giant, insane.

"My God! Was that the bear?"

"This person don't know. The bear, it was the bear. A little taste of blubber wake up the bear's stomach. Eh, eh," Edwardluk laughed nervously. Bear want to eat world."

"Give me my rifle," Dr. West demanded angrily.

"Eh-eh, he is only a bear." Edwardluk clicked the rifle's safety on or off; there was no way for Dr. West's ears to tell which. Edwardluk's voice diminished as he moved away. "Bear don't like man's smell. Once my brother's rifle don't work, and he lie still and bear sniff him and go away."

The snarling was the dogs.

"What are you doing?" Dr. West meant *don't leave me alone*.

"To shoot another seal. Dogs not fed enough to sleep, only enough to fight each other. This person must look for another seal." Edwardluk added with practicality: "Your smell will keep the bear away from the dogs. Before very long this person come back."

Dr. West groped on the sled for the harpoon shaft, clutching it.

"Best thing is sleep," Edwardluk's voice said, softer, but closer. Instead of leaving, Edwardluk squatted down so close Dr. West could feel his radiated warmth next to him and could hear his excited breathing.

"The important thing, will the whitemen like us?" Edwardluk blurted. "We don't harm anybody. We helped you. We want to help everybody because – we know. You frown, you twist when you sleep. But we sleep happy, all the same dream because we are here, we are there, we know why."

Edwardluk's voice hoarsened with emotion, with joy, and his hand gently closed on Dr. West's wrist. The great bear will come down when there are enough of us and—"

As Dr. West stiffened involuntarily, Edwardluk stopped speaking, as if sensing rejection. Again, Dr. West knew what Edwardluk was thinking: you don't like us. For 33 days Dr. West had been bombarded by the love and mythology of these people. They wanted – needed – to be liked.

If these people were not caged in this cultural sanctuary, Dr. West wondered, would they be scurrying door-to-door, knocking and disturbing housewives with a joyful apocalyptic message?

"He will come," Edwardluk's relaxing voice insisted, "when we have covered the world for him!" Edwardluk's grip tightened on Dr. West's wrist. "Our bodies will reward him for our birth." Edwardluk's voice rose in confidence and joy. "His great hunger is for us, for us. To this world and all worlds, he comes." He released his grip, standing up. His footsteps shuffled away over the ice. The dogs whined with hunger and hope of seal meat.

Through the wind drifted the distant grunting of the bear, and the wind hissed across the sled. Under the icy caribou skins, Dr. Wesley lay shivering. Eskimos say real life, dream life, begins while sleeping cold, dreaming cold, awakened into sleep like a wolf inhaling the scents, like a caribou hearing the most distant sounds, like a hand feeling …

V

During the third night he had camped with these people in an overcrowded tent where their stench congealed in leaden cold, his only desire had been for sleep. He had pushed away the smoothly bare arm. Tired and still apprehensive of venereal disease and lice, he did not want any anonymous girl. "Eh-eh," her faceless voice giggled. "Marthalik."

"Go away. I want sleep." But with warming excitement he soon became a lover of an intensity he had never experienced. His mounting ego said: Superman, you're getting out of it what you put into it. But he overpraised himself. Smooth-bellied and moving indescribably, Marthalik was the lover, he discovered.

In Marthalik's arms he dreamed the bear was approaching.

He laughed in his sleep. Unique. Marthalik might have become his Cleopatra, his Goddess Calypso who imprisoned

Ulysses in her island bed. He might have become an odd wanderer with an Eskimo wife. But when he went out to help search for Edwardluk's "brother", Marthalik had not accompanied him. She was not feeling well. Thinking of her warmth, he had trudged away with a dozen Eskimos. Camped in the cleft of a cliff, Edwardluk had persisted in offering his sister or his wife; Dr. West had been too sleepy to recognize which. Worn by Edwardluk's generosity, anxious not to hurt anyone's feelings, Dr. West said: "Oh, hell," and embraced her. Wonderful surprise! She was as wonderful as Marthalik. They all were. These wonderful women could conquer the world. He laughed in his sleep.

Even on the 23rd day, when he noticed that Marthalik, his first slender girl of the 3rd night, now appeared slightly thick-waisted and heavy-gaited, he could not foresee the reason the age population curve in this encampment was skewed so dramatically to children and babies.

During the 33rd night, a girl gave birth to a son. Dr. West tried to believe he confused one girl with another. They all looked so much alike. This girl could not be Marthalik. Holding her mewing baby under her chin, smiling proudly, she reassured him. "Eh, this person is Marthalik."

Her baby appeared to be a typical Eskimo baby fathered by an Eskimo, with a Mongoloid Blue Spot near the base of the spine. And even Eskimo babies were born with blue eyes. He kept telling himself he could not be the father. Marthalik could not be the mother. This was a full-term baby, which should take approximately nine months. A thirty-day gestation period should be impossible for a human being. It would be catastrophic for humans en masse.

These people cannot be Eskimos. What are they?

S hivering into wakefulness, awakened by whining dogs, Dr. West sat up on the anchored sled. The grunting sound, like an approaching hog, was the polar bear.

With his finger and thumb, Dr. West peeled one eyelid open and gasped with pain, stabbed by the blinding white light. His eyes flooded with tears. Along the sled he groped for the two harpoons.

"Edwardluk!" He shouted. The vast emptiness of sea-ice swallowed his voice and returned it, like a false echo of the grunting bear.

His hand gripped the harpoon shaft. Best weapon for a blind man? To his own surprise he laughed. A bit shrilly, but he laughed. Turning his head to follow the pig-like noises of the bear, he extended the harpoon. "Come on you invisible spook! I'm a man, not a seal."

His pounding heart, his surging adrenaline, had given him back his warmth, his liveness. He laughed, surprised he was not afraid.

Much closer than before, the bear growled.

The dogs yelped, violently thrashing the anchored sled, concealing any sounds of the bear.

In this uncertain moment Dr. West reevaluated. Those dogs were straining to escape. Escape was simple, even for himself!

His atavistic flow of courage froze. With the hurried gasps of a civilized man, Dr. West dropped the harpoon and unsheathed his short-bladed skinning knife. Of course the dogs would run; he thought they would drag the sled away, carrying him.

The bear growled.

Tight-muscled with fright, Dr. West lurched across the straining sled, fumbled back along the rail until his hand found the tight anchor strap. His knife slashed.

The strap broke, the lunging dogs yanking the sled from under him. He fell on his elbow on the ice, momentarily stunned by his stupidity as the clamor of the fleeing dog team faded into the distance.

He couldn't escape, he thought. Was he predestined to—?

"Edwardluk!" Dr. West started to rise and was warned by a cavernous growl.

He remained in a crouching posture, turning his head in the direction from which the sound had emerged. He was facing upwind, and an odor of rotting meat became noticeable, but now he couldn't hear the bear. The bear must be motionless, staring at him.

Gradually, Dr. West sank down on the ice, his knife hand under his shoulder as he flattened out on the ice, his vulnerable stomach pressed against the ice, his legs pressed together, his shoulders hunched protectively about his neck. His chest pressed against the ice, his heart thudding against the ice. He could hear the hiss-hiss of its breathing, the bear's shuffling advance.

Dr. West made no new attempts to open his eyes. He tried to see backward into his concrete-block cottage in California. It became a sunlit fortress. Behind the locked door, behind the multicolored dusty books on the top shelf, lay his .44 magnum Ruger Blackhawk revolver, heavy hog-leg-action revolver, its gleaming thick cylinder stuffed with six bullets looking fat as thumbs, packed with explosive emptiness.

The bear snorted. Motionless on the ice, Dr. West suppressed his breathing. He remembered real Eskimo hunters laughing at how they had behaved in such situations. Prostrate before their bears, they had lived to joke. "Don't breathe," Eskimos would say. "Bear never kills a dead man." The polar bear's stench engulfed him. Above him poised the hiss-hiss of its breathing. There was a gurgling sound, the ravenous contractions of its digestive system.

As forcibly as the blunt end of a baseball bat, the polar bear nosed his thigh, trying to turn him over.

Desperately he wanted to lunge away but lay in fear the bear's quick paw would smash him like a seal if he moved.

He wanted to leap away with a nightmare shriek as the bear's nose clubbed his thigh, his hip, shoving to turn him over, to expose his vital belly. Resisting, Dr. West tried to sag against the ice, to keep his belly down.

With an eager grunt and a series of hisses, the bear's nose burrowed under him, pushing up his hip. He twisted, was clamped –

The shriek and muscular spasm ballooned to his consciousness. His thigh, in the bear's jaws! With the squalling vitality of any animal being devoured alive, the former Dr. West writhed, striking the knife blade across the hard muzzle of the polar bear.

With a startled woof, the bear's jaws opened. Dr. West's body rolled away slashing the air and screaming defiance like a cornered animal. Backing away, gasping, he hacked the air with the knife while the shuffling sounds of the bear departed.

He became aware of the throbbing of his thigh. Gummed eyelids torn open, he faced blindly into the whiteness and listened through his own harsh breathing for the silent bear, then remembered who he was.

Dr. West's fingers explored the slippery twitching remnants of his thigh muscle. Hard-jawed he tourniqueted his belt around his thigh and gasped.

"Edwardluk," he gargled. "Edwardluk, Edwardluk!" he yelled.

There was no Edwardluk. "Edwardluk! Edwardluk!"

His voice thickened. His head seemed to sail away. He muttered and twisted, resisting. If he fell into shock, he thought in this cold he would be dead.

Dead, dead, irretrievably dead. All gone. Finished. Nothing.

From hissing wind emerged an approaching scraping sound. Edwardluk's voice wheezed, "Dogs turn away from water too late. Sled float. Curly tail drown. Loafer drown." All Edwardluk could talk about was the dogs. "Hump drown. Wind Runner drown." Edwardluk slid darkness and warmth down over Dr. West's hidden shoulders; Edwardluk was giving him his outer parka. "White Eyed drown."

Edwardluk was prodding his leg, wrapping his leg in something jelly-like within wet fur. "Fished out dogs. Cut up. Eh-eh," Edwardluk laughed feebly, "much good dog meat for everyone. This person cut open Wind Runner and White Eye for bear."

With crunching sounds, Edwardluk was breaking apart the sled, rebuilding it into a tiny man-sled. Gently, Edwardluk's hands tied Dr. West on the sled.

B lind, Dr. West knew they were microscopic specs in the enormity of sea-ice, shore-ice, and ice-shaped mountain islands.

"We go!" With a grunt, Edwardluk strained at the harness. For Dr. West, jolting hours moved through chills and sleep and fever, becoming days of blind agony without end.

Edwardluk's voice tried to soothe. "Eat-eat." He was pressing chewed dog meat into Dr. West's mouth.

Edwardluk would shout: "Ha! Forward, dogs!" while his stubby legs would tramp forward, endlessly dragging the man-sled with its raving burden, Dr. West.

"The bear," Dr. West would gasp. "Got to warn them." The Canadian Cultural Sanctuary Commission became twelve pairs of eyes surrealistically floating in a jury box. "Please believe me." *The population pressure among nations, in the amoeba-like growing struggles of the population masses of the world, these multiplying Eskimos will be the bomb for whatever nation makes use of these.* "Believe me, they're not Eskimos."

In his delirium, Marthalik's face rose smiling. He clung to her body. The droning of an airplane transformed snowflakes into parachutes drifting down with swaying food packages. As absurdly as Pop Art, these were paint-labeled FAMILY ALLOWANCES, swaying back and forth. Massive jaws crunching.

"Too many Eskimos." For these happy people, what did the bear symbolize? "Don't feed the bear!" he shrieked.

Giggling Eskimo women stuffed ovulation-suppressant pills into their ears. Their bellies inflated. The Earth tipped. From the darkness of space opened the jaws. "The bear!" he shrieked.

In more lucid moments, Dr. West clutched his swollen thigh and thought what a good man Edwardluk was. Laughing, straining, uncomplaining, that was the Eskimo image. They were cheerful people who fought no wars. It was true. So true. Men of goodwill all over the world would not let the Eskimos starve, no matter how many Eskimos. . .

VI

T he headwind carried the smell of fuel oil smoke, the barking of dogs.

"Carry the poor bloke into the storehouse where it's dark. I'll take the rag off 'is blinkers. Coo! Eyes like bloody sores!" The man's voice was the perpetual employee, Dr. West thought dazedly, another Englishman imported to Canada in the population struggle.

The French-speaking Canadians were outbreeding the rest two to one, gaining numerical control despite English immigration. French separatists no longer spoke of separations but of French as the required language in all of Canada's schools. Dr. West's eyes throbbed like hammer blows into his skull. His snow-blind eyes–

"Kerosene eyedrops, I always says," the ex-Londoner's voice was croaking. "Ere comes the Commissioner. Kerosene eyedrops for snow-blindness."

"No, wait!" Dr. West gasped. "Leave my eyes alone. I'm a doctor. I need special treatment. I must be flown to a hospital with – with Edwardluk."

"If you're a doctor, where's your kit?" The Cultural Sanctuary Commissioner's voice accused. "You're another cultural smuggler. You smuggling bastards won't leave the world's best people alone, not for a minute. You're the third smuggler I've caught in my district this year."

"No steel fishhooks, no transistor batteries on 'im," the ex-Londoner protested. "Coo! Commissioner, look at his leg!"

The Commissioner evidently bent over Dr. West's leg because there was a retching sound.

"Gangrene."

"Dog bite him," Edwardluk's voice volunteered. "Bad leg. This person drag him on little sled – that many sleeps." Edwardluk must be holding up stubby fingers, feigning ignorance of counting. "Dogs drown. This person drag him all the way from Mountain Bay."

"Thom Bay? That's an extremely difficult and hazardous—my man, you've completed an epic journey!" The Commissioner panted with pleasure. You're a hero."

He must be shaking Edwardluk's hand, as Edwardluk giggled with embarrassment. "Pulled whiteman long way. People hungry. He say much food here."

"No one will starve," the Commissioner said warmly. "Emergency Family Allowances will be authorized. Survival is always more important than 100% self-sufficiency. If necessary, we'll even paradrop a Family Allowance for every Family Head on the Boothia District Roster!"

"Eh-eh?" Edwardluk's voice laughed in confusion. "Will you help us? Many-many people hungry!" Edwardluk must be spreading his stubby arms. "Many people. Here his marker-book."

"I'll be damned!" From the sounds, the commissioner must be thumbing through Dr. West's notebook.

"He count people. Say not enough seals," Edwardluk expounded. "He count babies. Say more hungry quick."

"We'll make our own population survey. This man evidently is deranged. He appears to be dying."

"We help whiteman. He say all whitemen will like us because we help him." Earnestly, Edwardluk must be pressing his hand on his chest. "This poor person carry whiteman all this way. Pull sled like dog," Edwardluk laughed nervously.

"You're a better man than the whitemen!" The Commissioner was bubbling with enthusiasm for his Eskimos. "You've made an epic journey; there will be food for everyone. Boothia District will gain proper notice if you will speak about that on the C.B.C. The telly, the picture box. Tell them of the hunger."

"People hungry," Edwardluk repeated wistfully enough to melt the hearts of any TV audience. "Babies hungry."

Dr. West gritted his teeth. There was no use attempting to speak now. The Commissioner would not listen because he was in no mood for an "attack" against the Eskimos. Later he would emotionally reject unpleasant facts. Finally, when the Canadian Cultural Sanctuary Commissioner's noses were rubbed in the evidence, in the sinister implications of a one-month gestation period, both the Commission and the Canadian Government would temporize.

Or so Dr. West thought.

"Forcible birth control?"

"Surely not in a free nation! No matter what you say, they're as human as I am," the Commissioner would protest. "What would you wish us to do, let these good, happy, cooperative people starve? The real moral issue becomes GENOCIDE!" Dr. West's thoughts had a dreamlike reality.

"Coo! Is he dying?" said a voice which penetrated Dr. West's delirium.

He realized Eskimos also had Asian identifications. Dr. West dreamed the U.N. General Assembly with outraged shouts and dark faces rising against a rumor that Canada was planning "Eskimo family limitation." "Sterilization!" "Imperialist Suppression!" To aid the starving and disadvantaged Eskimos, the Chinese Federation of Nations would offer Cultural Assistance. Roaring airplanes from Asia, from Europe, from embarrassed America would parachute food throughout the spreading Arctic while the people multiplied and multiplied.

"Eh-eh, we fill the world," Edwardluk explained weeks ago with lovable simplicity, "until bear comes."

Death gnawed at Dr. West's leg, and he tried to sit up while Edwardluk's gentle hands held him down.

"Must speak," Dr. West gasped. *I must live.* "I must speak."

"You sleep now," Edwardluk was whispering, holding him down. "He come."

In his delirium, Dr. West could hear the galactic running of the bear.

PART 3: INTERPLANETARY TALES

HARANU

Written in 1950 in Miami, FL
Setting: On Mars, with an Earthman,
his dog, and a Martian

The moss flats curved beyond the horizon in all directions, their loneliness broken only twice, once by the straight, fern-edged line of a canal, centuries untended, and again by a shocking rectangular scar, a newly spaded garden patch. The moss had already soothed the dugout cabin's roof gray-green again, and now it imitated the chimney's smoke with little plumes of fog.

As the black earth foamed up with the gusto of a miniature volcano, Tip crawled closer on his belly, canines bared in grinning anticipation. There was an underground raider beneath the onion sprouts. Tip's snowy white tail wagged gently against the wind off frigid Mars Astral. Five generations of ancestors, carefully directed in their mating by men, had made it a fluffy bottlebrush long as his body—a muffler and nose-warmer for nights in the snow. He resembled a huge, deep-chested arctic fox.

The first dog upon Mars had run a few steps before his plastic-enclosed master, then fallen gasping upon the red cinders of Sinus Mariani. But five generations had genetically weaned Tip from even a daily oxyhemoglobin capsule. Physically at least, he was what the pallid men encased in the smog-wreathed city beyond Iron Plateau termed "integrated fauna." But the Martians, huddled in tarpaper barracks on Hellespontus Reservation, would have shaken their heads, opened their delicate hands, perhaps smiled a little with their huge amber eyes.

Tip was salivating now, stiffening as he sprung back, his muzzle like an egret waiting for minnows to rise. His ears laid into his fur, as his pulsating nostrils fished for the scent of marmoles in the confusion of damp earth smells, decaying moss roots, and newly bitten onion bulbs. Transparent soil-crabs were squeezed from their burrows by the marmoles' vigorous rise from the depths.

A soundless growl vibrated in his chest. He was the killer, the dominator, one of three conflicting roles his instinct and training had opened for him. At the other extreme, he was a wagging parasite, his great liquid brown eyes always locked on Gordon, his backbone curved in a nervous wiggle. Rarely, he knew peace in between. That was when he walked alone and quiet over the moss flats when, as the Martians say, his heartbeat was in tune with the planet.

Now he was hot-bellied with hunger. But even as he struck, he realized the marmole scent wore a sour skin. His jaws clamped not on wriggling, salt-flowing warmth, but cold, smooth strength that left a sour splash across his tongue as the creature tore loose from his incisors with a muffled and manlike shriek.

Backward Tip leapt, from a hand, long palmed, twice the length of an Earthman's. It was pale around its blue puncture wounds, yellow calloused, with nails like dirt-caked shovels. Tip fled, tail pressed hard against his belly, into his opposite role.

"Don't scratch the door down old boy, I'm coming." Gordon caught him in his muscular arms and squeezed out the trembling. His master had the delicious odor of bubbling stew, pipe smoke, salty sweat, and newly sanded magony roots.

"What are you afraid of boy? I don't hear any copters. According to my watch, the New Pittsburgh Afternooner doesn't send you under my bed for twenty minutes yet."

Gordon rolled backward onto the wood-shaving littered floor and pulled the dog across his barrel chest. He was a one-capsule-a-day man, conceived on Earth, but dragged feet first and squalling into the thin atmosphere of Mars. The domed cities had grown with his youth. But with the evaporation of the last snowfall, he had walked out of their mechanical harbor and started over again. His red beard, forty years away from his protesting entry on Mars, made Tip sneeze.

"What's wrong with you! Have you been hunting marmoles again? Serve you right if a big one gave you a scare. They were here first. Let them gobble up a little rent."

Tip wriggled with embarrassment at the teasing tone of Gordon's voice. He was his master's flawed mirror now. Gordon rubbed Tip's ears affectionately and he began to pant. This was ecstasy.

But the man lost interest. He rose and critically eyed the abstractism that had half-emerged from the strangely spiraling magony root. He started his vibradrill again.

The whine of steel on steel, the nervous crackling of electricity made Tip lose interest too. The machine filled him with disgust. It cut him off from Gordon. In a small way it cut him off from the planet, as the winnowing screech of the New Pittsburgh Afternooner would cut him off. He knew instinctively that it was coming and trotted only to his nearest watering post.

When the Martian night struck swiftly through the feeble shield of atmosphere, the cold crowded around Tip and made ghosts rise from his jaws as he crunched the charcoal biscuits. He growled contentedly. The memory of that cold, smooth hand tumbled backward behind the sweet juice in his mouth after Gordon's "come and get it" shout, and the late afternoon horror of the jetcopter. He carried the last biscuit over to where he could feel Gordon against his shoulder while he crunched.

Gordon's match flared. His pipe wheezed, lowering a prickly ribbon of smoke to Tip's nostrils. But the dog didn't mind. It was part of Gordon.

"Old boy, if I could stalk the flats and canal heads like you, secure that I was part of nature, if I could find peace, screwed tight into the world like a dog. . ." Gordon whispered in his ignorance as he wandered outside. He thought the almost equally alien Tip was his link with Mars. Sometimes he called Tip "my hope," whatever that meant. Somberly he watched Phobos' perpetual journey through the stars. That restless moon would pass by again before night faded. The night wind shattered through last year's dry ferns.

Gordon noticed the shadow before Tip scented its sour fear. Hulking from the fern breaks that edged the canal, dragging its arms like broken wings, it shuffled through the flowering bean rows with a ripping sound. Another followed, and another, closer and closer in the darkness until the dog's uncertain growl leapt into a frightened spasm of barking. Unsure whether it was his leg or the dog against it doing the shivering, Gordon kept drawing on his pipe. A backward glance told him shadows had risen magically from the earth between him and the cabin door. He owned no weapon.

His hasty grab for Tip's collar had the wrong effect. His touch was the inoculation of courage that made Tip lunge forward, dragging Gordon onto his elbows and knees. Tip's second lunge hurtled him free. Head low to the ground, the dog charged a dozen yards before he realized his master was not beside him. Then his growl curdled. He began a cautious withdrawal that degenerated into flight as those in the shadows squealed and waved their arms. They chased him to his stronghold between Gordon's legs. Crowding dangerously close, they seemed to be pointing, to be directing their anger at the dog.

Although they stood no higher than Gordon's chest, neither is a bull orangutan tall but still frightening. Their shoulders were powerfully broad, sloping directly from their smooth, earless heads. Their rounded snouts and cartilaginous foreheads gave them a reptilian appearance that was belied by their steaming breath and marmole-like squeals. With obvious intelligence, they nudged a small one until it edged closer and extended its arm.

When Gordon saw the swollen toothmarks there, he inadvertently glanced at Tip. At this they squealed in unison, and a big one lunged at Tip. In the instant Gordon checked his fist, he remembered them. The Borrons, the burrowers—were they from a Martian folktale, or something more concrete from Martian archaeology? As the big one swung its claws at Tip, Gordon shouted: "Muna haranu. Unam rananarey?" Have peace. What have we done?

But the Martian words had no effect, as sour, earth-caked bodies overwhelmed the man and his dog.

Above Tip's snarls, above squeals of rage and pain, a shriller squeal commanded. As one, the mole-handed ones disengaged. Like boys spotted beneath a farmer's apple tree, they sidled off in all directions, leaving a runway for a thin hurrying figure.

The Martian wore his nakedness like a golden cloak. Gliding his delicate fingers along his rudimentary forehead keel in a characteristic gesture, he spoke gently, in English more cultured than Gordon's.

"Really, you must excuse the Borrons. Although they are my friends and hosts, I must say they are an incredibly stupid horde. Knowing I would disapprove their revealing their last pitiful numbers to men, they nevertheless slipped away, intending to demand a settlement for the injury I presume your dog inflicted. But they've exchanged one bite for dozens."

He smiled as Tip sniffed his knee. "In their ignorance they did not consider how they might communicate with you. Often they lose their small wits when confronted with a new situation, and regress to violence." His lips made a gleaming curve in the darkness. "Like certain gentlemen from a third planet."

Gordon had no need to be reminded. As a young man, he had helped hunt the Martians into reservations. This Martian was a fugitive, Runeya Huranu Mana, one-who-seeks-the-pulse-of-the-planet. But there was nothing to fear; the Martians worship haranu – peace.

"Come to the warmth of my hearth," said Gordon. Now it was his turn to smile: "and bring your friends." He had not been surprised at the Martian's elegant vocabulary. Within a month after the first rocket landing on Mars, its gentle, amber-eyed people had conversed with nervous explorers in perfect English, Swedish, and Russian. Yet now, sixty years later, Earth philologists still could not speak to them in what they fondly imagined was Martian without arousing tolerant smiles. If the Martians had not revered the poet and philosopher rather than the strong-man and scientist, the Earth-Mars invasion might well have been the reverse.

Gordon's kindling of the fire brought nervous squeals from the Borrons, who stood together in the shadows, and a slight shudder from the Martian sitting cross-legged beside Gordon's magazine rack.

"Really, I appreciate the warmth, but somehow even after sixty years my body still wants to flee from fire. I am still a young man and far from haranu, but I think my forefathers on the reservation conceal the same revulsion to anything so alien as combustion in oxygen."

The fire bounced gleams of itself from the surface of the vibradrill. The Martian averted his head and shuddered visibly. "I cannot suppress it. No doubt your machine is beautiful to you, but to me, a Martian, it is fearful and grotesque. It is a single-willed dwarf, noisy with life yet unalive. To me, it's as incomprehensible as some of our mind tricks would seem to you, therefore terrifying, even obscene.

"Take patience for me, Earthman. For many seasons I have not spoken a symbolic language, and an indulgence of my people is in twining word symbols, jungles of them. But now I will become precise.

"I am Verymoon, a wanderer beneath Phobos, a seeker of harmony. I speak for my hosts the Borrons." His fingers glided down his forehead keel. "Do you know who they are? Borrons is only a word we Martians made for them. But your paleontologists know little more than that. They classify them as extinct burrowing carnivores. They gave them more words in something called Greek, word saying: naked-badger-who-stands-erect-like-a-man. This is like the story of the Martian poet-taxonomist who collided with a young earth woman in the dark and gleefully exclaimed, 'Betannon! I have discovered a Two-Nosed Archinor.' Nothing could be further from the truth. The Borrons are people like we Martians are, intelligent in their own way and with a deep appreciation of life.

"Yet when we were a young people, ignorant of the symbiotic nature of all life, we hunted them down with sticks, penned them on reservations where we could watch them die with scientific interest, trying to force their lives into our molds. Only a handful escaped. They fled underground, where they adapted themselves physically as you can see. Originally, they closely resembled us – and culturally – and they domesticated the marmole. Perhaps our treatment of them is a cause of what has since been visited upon us." The third lids veiled across the Martian's huge amber eyes.

"In any case, these few behind me are the last of the Borrons. The marmole herd is their life. Your companion's inroads upon it, rather than his undoubtedly accidental attack on the small Borron, is the basic cause of their hostility."

He stroked Tip, who amazingly— as he was ordinarily shy with strangers—snuggled against the Martian's skeletal chest. The dog thumped his tail on the floor, for the Martian emanated the delicious odor of sardines.

"What is it called?"

"Tip."

"Tip, the Borrons say you must not harm their marmoles or they shall drag your body into their holes and grow fat upon it. And they will drive your Earthman from the land."

The Martian turned his face to Gordon. "Does he understand my words? Or must you tell him in some personal way?"

Gordon shook his head. "There is a wide canal between dogs and men. We can only think and speak together of simple things that are there before us, not too far in the past, not too far in the future. If I struck Tip now for biting the Borron, he would not know why I was angry with him." Gordon snapped his fingers at the dog, but Tip would not leave the Martian. "He does not understand that what his nature wants him to do could be wrong. I have shouted at him so that he cowered at my feet. Twice I have tied dead marmoles to his neck, but he continues to do as his nature commands. He does not understand.

"Hunting marmoles is a big part of his life," Gordon continued. "Not only does it satisfy his instinct, he takes pride in defending my vegetable garden. If he could not hunt, he would be like the moss without the sun. His sorrow is mine, but I will try to make him understand."

"I too would be his friend." The Martian rubbed his cheek against Tip's shoulder. The dog flicked his tongue against the Martian's arm. Verymoon smiled. "You will pardon me, but I feel less cut off, more haranu, when your dog is between us, Earthman."

He looked up quickly. "But I have a feeling that machines are not so much in your mind as they are in most Earthmen's. Perhaps you were trying to cross to our side of the canal. Perhaps you someday will reach the edge and feel...." The Martian blinked and squeezed Tip until the dog's tail hammered on the floor. "...there is no word."

He rose gracefully, and the Borrons crowded behind him.

"We will go. Do not tie Tip too much. I myself would rather be nonexistent than on the reservation. But perhaps he too can find his own solution. All living things possess a will. One night I shall come back and try to cross to his side of the canal."

Tip's nights and days were spent straining at his harness rather than in search for an ultimate solution to a problem he did not realize existed. He howled, crunched the iron chain, and spoiled Gordon's sleep. When he remembered the delicious odor of the Martian and thought he smelled it on the wind, he wagged his tail, but tugged harder. The warm feel of wriggling salt-bleeding marmole was perpetually in his mouth.

Gordon, however, had conceived a possible solution. When a small trading copter lowered itself beside his dugout, he purchased four alarm clocks.

These he soldered into three-dimensional wire frames. The hum of the electric soldering iron made Tip whimper, but that was nothing to his yelping terror when one of those alarm clocks jangled.

Fingering his beard, Gordon smiled and shook his head. "That's an infernal machine all right, but this is one time your fear may be your salvation. Mine too. Now if Verymoon would only return..."

But the wind did not bring the sardine odor of the Martian. Only soil-crabs, marmoles, and other tiny creatures moved across the moss flats. They scurried quickly, for the dry chill of approaching winter was curling the ferns like brown clock springs. Hoarfrost glistened on the flats till noon. And when Gordon took the thin and snappish Tip for a walk along the canal bottom, he found the boisterous stream down there had dwindled to a scum of ice crystals.

The expanding polar cap sucked the moisture from the air and gave nothing in return.

Shapeless, scuffling tracks showed where the Borrons had crept down in the night to scrape up life-sustaining scum ice. Gordon often stared at the moist circles in the canal walls, revealing freshly plugged holes. But he did not attempt to contact the Borrons. Their thought and language barriers would more likely evoke hostility than cooperation. Of the Martian there was no sign.

One day at noon, the first dust storm howled up from the south. It sanded the windows, spit through cracks and left a yellow ochre world when it departed north.

Tip stopped sneezing long enough to strain at his harness. His skin showed red through his yellowed fur where the leather straps had chafed. Growling to himself, he tried to back out of the harness. He was almost thin enough.

A shrill whistle made him whirl. There, sitting boldly up right beside its hole—a withered onion stalk twitching between its jaws—was a marmole. With a gurgling roar, Tip hit the end of his chain, spun and to his great surprise fell backward on his tail. He was up in a flash and off, a comet leading a trail of dust. Of course the marmole ducked into his hole. But as the dog skidded to a stop, another marmole darted from the stalks almost at his feet. He had cut it off from the hole. The glorious chase was on.

It veered from side to side so that he overran it. His jaws clicked on empty air. But he was after it again. Long before it neared the hole, it had to dodge. Again Tip's jaws clicked, and he ran the marmole toward the canal. Momentarily he lost it in the ferns, but its dry rustling gave it away. As he lunged, it darted over the edge.

Landing with an explosive woof, he chased it through the scum ice, up an incline of fresh earth and into a faintly sour-smelling passageway. But the odor of marmole was too hot in his nostrils for him to hesitate about that.

Although the metallic whine of the vibradrill cut off Gordon from the world, he looked up, as though something had happened.

Am I becoming clairvoyant as a Martian?

He rushed out the doorway without bothering to glance at the empty harness. He chased the dog's running footprints through fresh dust, veered where they veered, crashed through ferns, and rode to the bottom of the canal on the seat of his pants. Rising, he stepped over dust-filled day-old Martian tracks, making his own trail of dirty boot prints across the ice while sending his whistle echoing.

Surprisingly, the dog's tracks ascended the dirt pile then vanished against the wall of the canal. He realized the Borrons had filled in their tunnel behind the dog. Frantically he dug into the hard-packed plug with his hands, then with a stiff root. He was breathing hard by the time he wormed his head and shoulders into the sour-smelling darkness. There was no answering bark to his whistles and shouts.

He was very frightened; he had sometimes dreamed of dying with his head caught in a small dark place. But he had to climb inside. As he wriggled through the earth, he heard and felt small furry things scurrying before him. Breathing hard, for the air was foul and weak, he crawled as fast as he could. Every moment he expected to feel the sharp claws of a Borron.

When an angry squeal sprayed spittle on his face, it was almost a relief. Curling up to protect his face and belly, he gasped repeatedly: "Verymoon? Haranu, Verymoon! Haranu!"

More squeals. The Borron ceased its mauling. They were all around him now. Nudging him with their foreheads, they drove him into a dead-meat smelling place where furry little clawed things leapt on him unafraid. He sat up, cautiously protecting his face and throat with his hands, and shouted for Verymoon.

A low whimper replied.

"Where are you, Tip?" he called.

But they wouldn't let him move. Squealing in all keys, they seemed to debate his fate.

"Verymoon," he shouted. Squeals and echoes of squeals mocked him. The Borrons made no response to his words and invisible gestures. The Martian was his only hope. For a long time, he sat listening to Tip whimper somewhere close by. Sometimes he thought he heard the shrill commanding squeal of Verymoon, but it was always the squeal of a Borron scrambling in from a faraway passage to join the convention.

Perpetual squealing and occasional sneak blows—not hard, just enough to torment—made his forehead burn with anger at his helplessness. The futility of his lack of strength, and his attempt to find peace on the moss flats, made his anger grow until he was ready to strike back at the next blow and blunder among them until they ended this farce with their claws.

"They are going to kill you," Verymoon panted unexpectedly close to his ear.

This bald repetition of what he already feared made Gordon snap caustically: "yes, haranu beats in all their breasts."

"But we must save Tip," the Martian whispered, unchastened.

"How?"

"I will speak with them."

After interminable squealing the Martian said: "They say they are going to kill both of you, their argument being: what will come will come. Since life from Earth and life native to Mars cannot live in peace, as Tip has demonstrated to them, they think it better to kill you in order to regain haranu as quickly as possible."

Gordon waited for his heart to stop drumming so loudly. "Verymoon, when I crawled in here, I had a plan. With your cooperation and theirs, I can end the basic cause of their hostility and make killing unnecessary." He spoke to the Martian for a long time, carefully explaining what he had in mind.

Verymoon exclaimed: "It is a cruel plan. But even if it is a lie, it may save you. Once outside you can flee to your domed city."

"I am not a liar."

"In any case I will treat with them. Even these poor borrowers do not lack that obliqueness of thought that you Earthmen term a 'sense of humor'."

The Martian silenced the angry squeals. Verymoon's voice rose and fell eloquently, then the Borrons chattered among themselves.

Verymoon told Gordon, "They will risk it. But if there's further trouble, they will come for you. Tip's forelegs are broken. I will help you carry him out."

In the clean air Gordon straightened up with a groan. Tip's tail beat feebly as Gordon loaded the dog across his shoulders.

"Go back to your domed city. If Tip cannot live there, I will keep him."

"No. I trust you will help me carry out the plan when Tip's legs have knit."

"I do not like it," the Martian replied. He turned before Gordon could thank him for saving his life, then vanished into the darkness of the burrow.

W hen Verymoon came again, the splints were off, and Tip could hobble to the end of his chain to greet him. The dust of departing winter swirled about them as they wrestled beneath the stars. When Gordon came out of the dugout, the Martian tossed him of the roll of marmole skins.

"It will be cruel," he said, but his feelings were diffcrent than a man's. He played with the dog so long that Gordon experienced a twinge of jealousy, as though the Martian were stealing his friend, his link with the planet.

After Verymoon departed, the dog was restless, but his legs strengthened rapidly. By the time the ferns unrolled fresh blooms of green, and mare's tails of ionospheric ice crystals from the evaporating polar cap made southward-moving shadows on the flats, he was tugging at his harness. He barked at the now insolent marmoles like the old Tip again.

Gordon weighted a white undershirt with a stone. Standing in the ferns at the edge of the canal, he threw the weighted shirt across the silt-darkened stream to an earth pile against the far wall. That night Tip began to snarl and whimper. He could smell a Borron out there in the darkness. Gordon hurried out and handed the Borron a package. After its hulking shadow had dropped over the edge of the canal, Gordon shook his head wearily before going inside to play with Tip.

The morning sun revealed a worried smile above his beard. He unharnessed the dog. "Go out and play Tip; you're on your own."

He felt like a Judas as the dog raced over the flats.

Tip sniffed the earth piles around old marmole holes. He danced with the wind, snapping joyously at spring soil-crabs. Having split their shells, they fluttered clumsily over the moss. Their iridescent wings crackled between Tip's teeth. When a marmole squeaked and showed his head, Tip charged the hole. After sniffing impatiently in the entrance, he backed away and waited, tongue rolling, tail waving in the breeze off Mars Astral.

The marmole was impatient too. It bobbed into his jaws. With a glorious crunch, Tip jerked its bony furriness from the hole. With horrible suddenness it jangled in his mouth. So great was his shock, his jaws froze about its metallic vibrations, and he rolled and thrashed a moment before he could shake it loose. Tail pressing against his belly, he streaked for the dugout.

Gordon crawled under the bed to lay beside him. Tip was an earthquake of fear.

It was two days before he would venture to the doorway. The other three alarm clock-stuffed marmole skins were never used. Tip had lost interest in hunting. He lost interest, period. He moped about Gordon's feet, even enduring the hideous whine of the vibradrill, until Gordon tripped over him and told him angrily to get out of the way. But the doorway was his outer limit.

"You're a neurotic creature!" Gordon exclaimed and tried to drag him for a walk. But the terrified dog snapped at him.

"Perhaps we should go back to the city," Gordon said.

But one night, when the flats were bright with the first ephemeral snow of summer – in winter the air was too cold and dry for snow—the Martian came. His inviting whistle made Tip tear at the door with his claws. When Gordon opened it, the dog streaked across the snow to greet the shadow. Together they raced through the ferns and disappeared over the edge of the canal.

Gordon stared at the empty flats for a long time before he went inside. He did not care to start his vibradrill just then.

Beyond the canal, where the wind tossed powdered snow against their eyelids, the dog and Martian romped together. Verymoon laughed like a man and threw puffs of snow at Tip. Rolling on the white blanket, he rubbed it all over his nakedness and Tip's soft fur until they looked like two snow creatures wrestling so violently, they seemed bound to melt.

When another Martian, a young female, rose from a moss-concealed burrow, Tip woofed and raced to greet her. The three of them raced Phobos towards the horizon.

"Hbuna pmana rumn?" she laughed.

"Pmana rumn Tip," Verymoon shouted and pinched her vigorously.

"Unam haruna!" she squealed.

Verymoon yodeled joyously and pursued Tip in constricting circles until Tip turned and chased him. After a while he led the dog and the female over canals strange to Tip, far away over the flats. The wind pursued them on their journey.

Building up the fire so its glow would show through the windows, Gordon zipped his jacket and stepped into the cold. Before he reached the ferns the wind turned and sprinkled his face with snowflakes. Stopping frequently to whistle and listen, he crossed the canal and advanced swiftly over the tracks of the Martian and the dog. Pocketing his numb hands, he swung a hopeless stare across the flats but kept moving into the wind.

When he noticed the footprints of a smaller Martian, he shook his head in wonderment, dislodging a miniature snowstorm from his beard. So other Martians were fugitives!

When the wind shifted to his back and the snow paused, he moved faster, occasionally trotting crisscross to relocate the trail. His vapor-wrapped whistle made a lonely sound.

Wading across a tributary canal, he shouted into the night. His breathing was quick; he'd forgotten to take his oxyhemoglobin capsule.

His whistle diminished to a peep. There was a throbbing pain beneath his heart, long before he made out the dark spots moving on the snow. The smallest of the those ran in his direction. But as Gordon yelled, it whirled and raced back to the other two who seemed to beckon to it. Gordon stuffed his hands back in his pockets and watched with humped shoulders as the dog vacillated, running a little way, then running back. Gordon would not yell again.

The snow flurried over the flats, obliterating spots. It whirled a cloak of blindness around Gordon's head and piled on it his head and shoulders. He stood motionless as a stump. Only the rising fog of his exhalations showed he was alive.

The quick, regular puffing of the running dog arrived long before the dog did. Gordon had plenty of time to open his arms. With a joyous yip, Tip leapt as high as his master's face and bestowed a juicy slap of his tongue. Gordon chuckled.

"Made your choice, eh. We'll find a substitute for marmoles, and Martians too."

Side by side they walked back through the snow toward the muffled light of the cabin.

MUTINY IN THE ORBIT OF URANUS

Written in Santa Barbara, CA, mid-1950's-60s
Setting: Outer Space in the Future

Like a sparkling salmon, the spaceship Explorer IX leapt across the black, star-jeweled sky and swirled around the planet Uranus in a series of contradicting ellipses to reduce its momentum.

From its plexide noseport, Commander Ross stared down at the distended, luminous cloud banks that had forever hidden Uranus from the eyes of Earthmen. Although the clouds looked harmless, vaguely reminding the Commander of green-stained mashed potatoes, he knew they were poisonous with radioactivity.

"In a few moments I shall be dead or a hero." He thought not at all of his crew.

Covertly brushing a bead of sweat from his upper lip, he pressed the landing initiator of the automatic pilot. Obediently the enormous spaceship nosed up in a gravity stall and slid stern-first into the clouds, its ramjets pushing desperately against the murderous gravity of the planet. He groaned as the Geiger count accelerated to a deadly scream, then shouted with joy as it subsided to a harmless, steady click. He realized radioactivity was but a shell around the planet. He pressed his cheek against the plexide. What was down there? Deserts of rock? Pillars of dust? Ice fields of frozen ammonia gas?

Then he gasped from sheer amazement, seeing beautiful green lakes freckled with tiny wooded islands. Struggling into his space suit, he declared: "I, Commander John Ross, have discovered a wonderful new world."

When the ship grounded gently on an island, something of the small boy in his nature made him shout through the intercom, "Men, there may be dangers here. As your captain, I order you to remain in the ship while I investigate." A twenty-first century Balboa, he wanted to be first.

He opened the airlock and dropped onto the spongy turf. To his surprise, gravity was no stronger than on earth. His wrist thermometer hovered at 62°F. The shadowless landscape was clearly lit by the glowing cloud banks.

Astronomers guessed wrong about Uranus, he thought. When they calculated its mass as 14.7 times that of earth, they had measured miles of clouds, then wondered why the planet's density was so low.

He scooped up a glove-full of dark rich earth. "Uranus, you are the new Earth. Your climate seems better, with twenty-four hours of daylight, steady temperature, no wind, and your warm cloud cover is better than any sun."

He whispered happily to himself: "I am the first man on Uranus."

Something touched his shoulder, and he jumped back. His expression contracted from open-mouthed surprise into a childish pout, for there before him stood a MAN.

The man extended his hand with an easy, muscular motion. He was neighborly-looking, with gray sideburns, faded khaki tight across his chest muscles, and courage-dark blue eyes.

Commander Ross self-consciously kicked sod with his boot toe and shook hands. The man grinned widely and pressed his forehead against the commander's helmet, shouting, "Come on out. Plenty of oxygen here."

Commander Ross spoke halfheartedly into his suit's tele-radio, "Come out men. But be on your guard." Then he allowed the man who had stolen his thunder to help him out of his space suit.

"How did you get here?" he blurted.

"I came on the Sky Dagger," the man replied, pointing to the lake where the needle-pointed nose of a fantastically obsolete spaceship protruded from the green water.

"Crashed, eh?" the commander mumbled absently. Then he did a doubletake and shouted: "Sky Dagger, that was the ship, Captain Rawn's ship, where the tube men mutinied. We've been hunting it for twenty years! We thought it must've become a satellite. Mister, you've got plenty to tell me and a Court of Inquiry, too!"

The man still smiled. "Will you accept my hospitality while we talk? My name is Paul Dixon."

The Commander nodded impatiently and shouted for a crewman to bring along a tape recorder. As he followed Paul Dixon, they passed a neat vegetable garden and a corral containing three green, bulging-eyed finned creatures as large as hogs and superficially resembling mudskippers. Alongside a long, low dwelling with walls and roof of green-growing sod, a clothesline sagged with diapers, rompers, and pink lingerie.

Inside, Paul Dixon offered the commander a yellow plastic swivel chair that had obviously been retrieved from the wreck.

"I signed on the Sky Dagger as Paul Smith, tubeman," he said.

"Mutineer, eh!"

Paul Dixon shook his head. "I was a secret investigator for the Global Council. Believe me, I did my best to prevent the mutiny."

He leaned forward and began to talk rapidly, earnestly, cathartically—he'd been saving up this talk for twenty years.

Paul's Story

I was a greenhorn as far as space travel was concerned, but the Global Council decided I was the man to investigate the uranium mining operations on Neptune. The Radium Trust, which operated the domed city and mines on Neptune, had become increasingly wasteful. There were rumors of corruption and graft—even treason. I was ordered to sign on one of Radium Trust's carriers as a tubeman. When we reached Neptune, I was to jump ship, then work in the mines while gathering evidence on the Q.T.

But I made a poor choice when I signed on the Sky Dagger. After boarding, I learned the tubemen had nicknamed it the Sky Stagger. Indeed, it staggered through the skies, bouncing my queasy stomach between my ribs and backbone. It was a flying coffin. It was one of those old exploratory ships now converted to a cargo carrier and had been cracked up a dozen times.

Although it constantly shed fins, blew out neutron tubes, and even poisoned two men, the Radium Trust wouldn't replace it. They spent their subsidies on fancy office buildings and fancier blonde stenographers.

You can imagine what sort of crew a junk heap like that would have. Most of the tubemen were convicts pressed into service. Captain Rawn was an old fussbudget who'd been a famous space explorer in his day, but, believe me, his day was long past. That old ironjaw was obsolete. Demotion to the lowly Sky Dagger kept an angry rod in his spine, but when he thought he was alone he'd slip out his false teeth and his back sagged into a tired S. He was an old man waiting for death.

The First Officer's spine was soft even in public; he drifted around the ship muttering to himself like a senile Hamlet. The Navigator – big brass of the Radium Trust—

had an advanced title: Astrogator. They thought naval titles were more dignified, more "traditional" as they put it. The Navigator was a young woman, good-looking. Imagine sending a woman officer clear to Neptune on her first voyage!

Still, she was the only competent officer on board. The Engineer had installed an elaborate distilling apparatus in his statement room, which he rarely left. The Communications Officer had just been unlucky in love, so didn't care what happened on board.

The journey to Neptune is the longest, most boring voyage within the solar system. To keep us from growing too bored, the Director of Radium Trust sent along two young men who were studying to be high officers of the Trust. Coincidentally, they were his sons.

Was he trying to make men of them, or murder them? After they discovered the delights of liquid dynamite dripping from the Engineer's still, they spent their more lucid moments trying to break into the Navigator's stateroom. They also picked fights with tubemen, then ran like little tattletales to the Captain when they got hurt.

To make our joy complete, the cook, a vanilla extract addict, couldn't pull himself together long enough to serve a passable meal to the officers. He'd conveniently collapse so the cross-eyed messboy had to prepare our slop.

One day, Garheim, unofficial leader of the tubemen, caught him boiling our beans in soapy dishwater. Garheim threw that boy into the airlock and would've pulled the switch that opened the outer door, exploding the boy in a vacuum, if I hadn't grappled with him.

Garheim was an ex-con who looked like a gorilla with a receding hairline. His temper was even uglier, and he didn't seem very bright. Arthur Hunt, the only tubeman who didn't look as if he'd rather stab you in the back than spit on you, said Garheim was rumored to have been a space pirate.

Mutiny seemed a fitting end to the Sky Stagger's logbook. That ship was a flying mistake. It wasn't a comfortable spinning-gravity ship with artificial gravity on its outer wall-walking services by centrifugal force. It was one of the few so-called magnetic-gravity ships, built in the early experimental years before they knew any better. Slice it lengthwise. The lower half contained ore-holds. The upper half had living quarters, control rooms and propulsion units.

Those electromagnetized floors were a poor excuse for gravity. We wore iron shoes to keep our feet down. But who could keep pillows on bunks, poker chips on tables, and food on forks? The air was always cluttered with things that got away.

The cramped staterooms were arranged along a dismal central corridor extending from the control room in the nose to the tuberoom and propulsion units in the tail. Peeling strips of gray paint hung like Spanish moss along its walls. Floors were bloody with rust. Doors, warped and creaking, opened onto the messroom, galley, cook's stateroom, tool room and two-cell brig.

Forward, well-oiled doors opened to the Captain's office and officers' staterooms. The tubemen bunked aft, along the tubes, where the endless whine of faulty machinery joined the tramp, tramp of iron shoes on iron floors in a blacksmiths' symphony.

But when tired enough, miserable enough, your ears grow deaf, and sleep is the jet-black hole you can pull in after you.

When we neared Mars' orbit, Garheim blundered into the captain's office. "Sir, I'm speakin' for duh men," he grumbled.

He wasn't speaking for me; I hadn't asked him to open his big mouth.

But he added, "Sir, dose tubes is gonna blow up. We gotta land to fix 'em."

The Captain shouted for the Engineer to come to the office and refute this claim. But the Engineer couldn't come; he was wrestling with the DTs. The Captain ordered Garheim to the brig for a week on food pills and water. He knew full well that if we landed on Mars, the tubemen would jump ship.

"I've never lost a ship," he rasped. "By all the stars, my ship goes to Neptune." To show us his iron wasn't rusted, he took away our smoking privileges.

Now, the Navigator not only had deep blue eyes—gentle lakes that made you stop breathing—she had an unruffled voice and protruding lower lip. When she ran interference for us with the captain, he gave back our cigarettes.

I think she was the only officer who realized these tubemen were dynamite: old dynamite, jiggle it, and it goes off. But they didn't take kindly to her. They felt vaguely angry at serving under a woman, no matter how pretty she was. I tried to act respectful, but sometimes I'd forget myself and act too friendly. Then she'd show me what a straight back she had, but I hoped she was hiding a smile.

After we passed Jupiter, I discovered that she hesitated to enter the tuberoom unless I was in there, for Garheim and several other men had grown disgustingly insolent. They'd found she would give them no more than a tongue-lashing.

They interpreted this as weakness, but it was part pity. Hardly a day passed that one of us wasn't burned reloading those ancient tubes. I have a beautiful scar on my hip where Garheim "accidentally" jolted me against the main burner. The Navigator came down to the tuberoom to dress my wound.

"Smithy," she said, "you've got to get out of this life. You're too decent a fellow to waste yourself here. Sometimes, when I listen to your voice, I think you're putting on an act. I think you're really an educated man." Then she turned red, then said no more. But I knew what she was thinking: he's committed a serious crime; that's why he's out here. He's a criminal.

I wished I could tell her the truth. I wished a lot of things.

Outside, Saturn painted a quarter of the black sky with gold and red. Swirling rings glinted in the distant sunlight; nine satellites trooped by in rainbow uniforms. But lifeless beauty fades to boredom, and boredom into sullen anger, winding like a clock spring ever tighter, and if you wind a clock too tight…

Beyond Saturn's orbit, Garheim broke the jaw of the elder son of the Director of Radium Trust, the one we called Fancy Pants. But the captain revealed an unsuspected sense of humor and sentenced Garheim to only two days in the brig.

This proved a serious blunder. Garheim now thought he could get away with murder. And he did. One sleeping period, I heard the outer door of the airlock open and close. The younger son of the Director was seen no more. The Captain ordered an inch-by-inch search of the ship, knowing quite well what had happened. Perhaps he was pleased? This was revenge against the author of his demotion. He made no serious effort to arrest the murderer.

If I'd been Captain, having no direct evidence against Garheim as a murderer, I still would have judged him for insubordination, disrespecting superiors, and habitual negligence. I would have tacked on to his offenses hanging laundry in the mess room, failure to shave his face or shine his boots, smoking while on duty, and drawing obscene pictures in the tubemen's head. I would have kept him behind bars till Neptune.

Garheim was a constant troublemaker. Without constant pushing from Garheim, the men would not have mutinied. Yet Captain Rawn did nothing. He was a great man once, but an old fool now!

One rest period, after I had finished defeating Arthur Hunt at chess, Garheim swaggered over.

"Play me, granny," he blustered, "I'll show you how chess is played."

I had to smile at this. I did not anticipate much of a battle from an ignorant tubeman who looked and acted like an inebriated gorilla. I was afraid I'd have to show him the moves of the various pieces. To my amazement, he developed his pieces skillfully, opening on a variation of the Ruy Lopez. However, as the game progressed, his attack became disorganized. He made several stupid oversights. I thought: *This ape has memorized an opening, but when he must depend on intelligence alone, he's an ape again.*

I played aggressively, losing two pawns unnecessarily. It was more than a game to me. It was a vicarious death struggle with my enemy—a means by which I might learn what sort of intellect lurked behind that stupid exterior. I butchered his pawns and bishops. He lost his queen by sheer carelessness. Just as I gained his last rook on an exchange, I realized to my horror that his knights were so well-placed that in two moves my king would be in checkmate.

Was it chance? Did he know? His mouth sacked open in an expression of utter stupidity, but he made the first move toward my king's downfall. I stared into his eyes, narrow, shiny black with triangles of red in the corners, no whites at all. He closed them, and, I swear it, he blushed red like a small boy caught in a lie. There was only one wrong move he could make. He made it! So I killed his knight, then easily went on to checkmate his king. But a nasty, frightening suspicion exuded cold sweat on my palms. Had he been playing cat and mouse with me?

As if to deny this, he angrily swept my remaining pieces onto the floor.

"You're a ringer," he grumbled.

And you are another, I thought. But I felt more like a mouse.

The next rest period, real trouble began. Hamlet— I always thought of the First Officer as Hamlet—came out of his reverie long enough to wander into the tubemen's head, where we were clustered in a circle shooting craps, which is quite a trick with no gravity.

"Well, I declare," he said, "I think you men must be gambling. Haven't you've been told gambling is never permitted on the spaceships of Radium Trust?"

One of the men tittered; we'd been gambling quite openly since the Sky Stagger parted from its step-off rocket.

"You, and you," piped Hamlet, selecting two men at random. "I think you should go to the brig, while I inform the Captain."

They looked to Garheim for advice, but his hand hid his face and his shoulders quivered with silent laughter. This was what he'd been waiting for. Finally he nodded for the men to obey Hamlet's order. They shrugged, clanked up the corridor to the brig, and locked themselves in. They didn't expect to be there long.

After supper, Garheim stretched himself and casually announced that he was going to see the Captain about Rod and Ed in the brig. Since the jaw-breaking episode, he had acted as if the Captain and he were buddies, so I thought he was going to diplomatically plead for the release of Rod and Ed. But I underestimated him. He had a more subtle plan.

When he returned, he seemed quite pleased with himself.

"Gimme time," he said, "I'll get those boys out yet, if the Captain don't kill us first, that is."

"What do you mean?" Arthur Hunt demanded.

"The Captain's got lots of big knives in his cabin. When I come in, he's sharpening 'em. Go home, he says, you are me buddy, but some of those guys I don't like. When the lights are out, I'm gonna go back dere and —."

Garheim drew his finger across his throat suggestively, then he strapped himself in his bunk, laughing.

"I'm glad I'm not some of you guys." From the expressions on their faces, I judged most of the tubemen took him seriously.

"What about Rod and Ed?" I asked.

"Duh Captain is tough on gamblin.' Dose boys is goners."

The next day, when Rod and Edward were not released, morale hit bottom. I went to the Captain.

"Sir, we wondered when Rod and Ed would be released."

"Release those two murderers?" He shouted, "You greenie, you're space crazy."

Murderers? I ran back to the tuberoom.

"Garheim told the captain that Rod and Ed shoved the Director's kid out the airlock," I blurted.

"Yoora liar," Garheim yelled.

"And you are a yellow, squealing rat," I replied.

He rushed me, then stopped in his tracks.

"You just wanna get me in trouble," he blustered. Leaning forward, he whispered: "You all know Rod and Ed is in duh brig for gamblin'. You saw 'em arrested." Then he whooped with laughter. "We can't do nothin' on this ship, not even shoot craps. All we can do is—" He smiled and drew a finger across his throat.

Those poor devils didn't know what to think.

The next work period, Garheim, Arthur and I were repairing the electromagnetic gravity floor of the messroom. It had short-circuited, so knives and forks floated about the room like asteroids. Suddenly Garheim grabbed Arthur from behind. Laughing, he plucked a knife out of the air and pressed it against Arthur's throat.

"I'm duh Captain," he roared. "Arthur is one of duh guys I'm gonna get."

"Stop fooling around," Arthur gasped.

"Arthur, you're as pale as a dead guy who got all duh blood drained out. Duh Captain says to me, duh first throat I cut is Arthur Hunt's."

"Watch this ape," I said, "he's working a war of nerves. And one day he's going to talk mutiny."

Later I overheard Garheim talking through the bars to Rod and Ed. "Boys, you been railroaded. Duh Captain says he's gonna get you court-martialed for gamblin' when we get to Neptune. You know what dat means? Ten years burnin' to death in duh uranium mines."

Around the mess table, while we were griping more than usual, Garheim banged his heavy fist on the table. He rumbled: "The lousy officers ain't the only guys eatin' good. I know guys who has champagne and sizzlin' steaks, and roast beef with duh juice running out, and caviar sandwiches, and beautiful Venus girls to serve it to 'em."

He waited for this utopian picture to soak in. Then he whispered, "Pirates."

"Pirates don't live long," I retorted.

He snorted: "Propaganda from duh Global Counsel. Gimme a ship, and a few guided rockets, and some brave guys who wanta make somethin' of themselves, like you guys. A pirate should clean up. Buy anything on Mars, no questions asked. Capture one ship and we can all take life easy."

I pushed back my chair: "So you finally got up the courage to suggest we seize the Sky Dagger, or didn't I hear you right?"

Thoughtfully, he screwed his finger into his ear. Then, I swear it, the gorilla blushed. He pushed back his chair and pointed his finger at me. "Smithy, are you suggesting mutiny?"

Then he threw back his head and laughed hoarsely in my face. "Duh dirty deal Captain give Rod and Ed is enough to make a guy talk mutiny. Mutiny ain't such a dirty word."

Then he frowned. I could almost hear his mind working. He didn't want to go all the way yet. "Who got duh dice? Damn brass hats and females ain't gonna stop me from shootin' craps."

"Now you're talking," exclaimed one of his buddies. Everyone looked relieved. But as I went out the door, someone said, "What do you think, Garheim —if we mutinied, could we beat 'em?"

Garheim was the puppet-master now.

I knocked softly on the Navigator's door.

"Come in Smithy," she said. "Don't stand so stiffly—at ease, sit down, forget I'm an officer."

I realized I'd never seen her with her cap off before. Her shimmering hair was upswept in the latest feminine fashion. She smiled self-consciously and ducked her head, and her small ears grew quite red. I listened to the blood thumping in my temples and forgot what I was going to say.

But it came back in a chilling rush. "Sir," I blurted, "Garheim has incited the tubemen to the verge of mutiny."

She showed no surprise. "I believe you. We recognize morale is low. But you must understand, Garheim is an old-time spaceman. Captain has great respect for him, since they went through the same dangers in the experimental days."

"Garheim never served under him before."

"Even so, Captain Rawn is convinced that Garheim is the only tubeman who'd be dependable and know what to do if we had one of those horrible accidents so common in the early days. He thinks Garheim's the backbone of the crew."

"Doesn't he realize," I said, "that Rod and Ed didn't shove the Director's son out the airlock? If he'd release them, one of Garheim's talking points for mutiny would be gone."

"But Garheim's story may be true; Rod and Ed are paroled murderers who were impressed for service on this ship. They're the most logical suspects."

I groaned. Garheim was always a move ahead of me.

"But Garheim told the crew that Rod and Ed are still in the brig for gambling," I insisted. "That's what's kept them stirred up."

That made her eyes widen. So I told her how Garheim said the Captain had gone crazy, saying he sat in his cabin sharpening knives, intending to cut the throats of the tubemen. She smiled at this. But when I jumped to my feet, she said, "Don't look so angry, Smithy. I believe you. Let's go see the Captain."

As we reached his door, she pressed my hand and whispered, "Be respectful Smithy, no matter what he says. I know you're a proud man, but remember, in his eyes you're just a greenhorn."

Greenhorn is right! In his eyes, I was beneath contempt, almost beneath listening to. He yawned and scratched his neck and peeked at a dog-eared picture magazine on his desk.

Finally, he chuckled dryly: "Me, cut their throats? Garheim isn't bright, but he'd never make up that silly a story. Greenie, you've got space fever."

I started to tell him the motives for Garheim's lies, that Garheim's stupid manner was a mask, a sham. But the Captain snapped: "You've wasted enough of my time. Any more troublemaking from you, and you'll sit out the voyage in the brig."

Angry futility fogging my brain, I marched into the corridor while the Navigator whispered, "Be careful, Smithy."

"Don't you think Garheim will knock me off for a stool pigeon?" I snapped, "Would that be a great loss?"

She flushed: "You forgot something."

"Oh. SIR, would that be a great loss, SIR?"

"Not to the ship it wouldn't," she retorted, and she stepped into her stateroom and slammed the door. That felt like a slap in the face. I walked back to the tuberoom, mentally kicking myself.

"There he is—the Captain's spy." Garheim jeered.

"Guess again. If I was, you'd have been thrown out the airlock long ago, you yellow rat."

I wanted him to fight me. Big as he was, I was going to put him out of commission. Without Garheim there would be no mutiny.

I called him every name in the book. He stood there, clenching and unclenching his hairy fists. I was making him lose face, but he was too yellow to fight, or too smart.

I walked up to him. What would he do if I hit him on the mouth? I didn't find out, because three of his buddies grabbed me from behind and held me while Garheim hit me. That's how he regained face. Before he could make me unrecognizable, several tubemen loudly protested and Arthur threw a chair.

So there was a pro-Smithy faction, too! It was worth a split lip to discover this. There seemed to be five of us.

When the messboy brought in our so-called food, a gummy stew that would not float off our steel plates, we ate silently, eyeing each other. Suddenly Garheim shouted with rage and pointed at his plate. His stew was moving. While we watched, he fished out an enormous cockroach.

"Dis is too much," he yelled, throwing the gravy-laden cockroach on the table. "Duh officers eat steak and give us cockroaches."

It was all too pat. There had never been a cockroach in the food before.

"You planted it there," I said, but I lost my four followers by that statement; they wanted to believe the officers served us cockroaches. With righteous anger, they shouted me down.

Garheim thumped his chest: "We'll show him who eats cockroaches, and who locks up who for shootin' craps. Remember Rod and Ed. We can't let down our buddies. Dat Captain can't cut our throats. Dose lousy officers and Fancy

Pants and dat cook who's too good to cook for us, we'll get 'em all. Everybody who got guts, stand up."

Everybody stood up except me.

"Mutiny means death," I said. "The officers have guns. You've got Garheim with his drivel about guts. Guts won't do you much good if you have to hold them in with your hands, after you've stopped a bullet with your belly. Suppose you capture the ship, which you won't—every space cruiser will be on your tail. They'll blow you apart, if Garheim doesn't double-cross you first."

Arthur and two others sat down.

"He's a spy," Garheim roared. "We can't lose. We outnumber him two to one."

"A typical Garheim lie," I retorted. I was stalling, hoping they'd cool off. "There's the Captain, First Officer, Navigator, Communications Officer, and Engineer. Add the cook, messboy, Fancy Pants and four of us here. That's twelve against you, with guns. You've got eight, without guns."

"You're not counting Rod and Ed," he yelled. "Remember dem?" Then he laughed without humor. "Look who he counts: a woman, a jerk with a busted jaw, some drunks and some old men. And you guys don't count at all. Dis mutiny's going to be unanimous. You're either with us, or dead."

Chairs scraped. Now only Arthur and I remained seated. I slid my hand down my hip toward my stubby, all-purpose spaceman's knife. But the scabbard was empty!

I tossed a look at Arthur, and we broke for the door. Someone grabbed my waist, but I kept driving. As I reached the door, Arthur cried out. I turned so savagely they fell back, and I fought my way toward Garheim. He lunged to meet me, and my fist skidded off his cheek. As his tree-like arms clamped about me, I clubbed his neck and kidneys and let him feel my knee. But as he reeled back, others piled on me, arms pinning mine, fists blinding my eyes, heavy boots kicking my kneecaps till I toppled.

A shot boomed. Guns leveled, the Captain, Navigator and Engineer stood in the doorway. From the floor, I shouted, "The mutiny has begun!"

The men climbed off my back and stood silent, hands in the air. For an instant, I thought I had won, the truth had won, and mutiny nipped in the bud. But Garheim was a move ahead.

"Sir, Smith went nuts and stabbed Arthur Hunt. We was tryin' to restrain him."

I twisted around. Arthur was spread-eagled on the floor, the handle of my spaceman's knife growing from his chest. Everybody started shouting at once. After a while, a hollowed out feeling of utter futility sucked even the anger from my protests. It was my word against Garheim and nine others. And it was my knife.

Rod and Ed were moved into one cell, and I was thrown into the other. But women are peculiar animals. The Navigator whispered through my bars, "I still believe you," when I hardly believed it myself anymore.

"Please do this for me," I whispered. "Lock the tuberoom door when you're sleeping. And carry your pistol at all times."

From my cell, I had an excellent view of the corridor. I resolved to keep watch. If the mutineers made a sudden attack, I'd shout a warning.

During the next working period, I heard metallic hammering rise from below, as if someone was opening the bulkhead doors connecting the ore-holds. With the doors open, a man could walk the length of the ship through the empty holds, then emerge through manholes in the tuberoom and into the control room. But the lid of the control room manhole was padlocked. Breaking it open from below would be noisy. And only one mutineer at a time could crawl through.

I realized if I shouted for an officer and asked him to investigate, and the crew was doing legitimate work down there, I'd be considered the boy who cried wolf. Later, if I shouted a real alarm, no one would believe me.

Later in the day, I saw Garheim grab the messboy, who'd lived in mortal terror since the day Garheim tried to eject him through the airlock. Garheim whispered in his ear for at least five minutes, while the boy's knees slowly buckled. He hung from Garheim's hand like a rag doll.

When the boy slunk past my cell, I called out to him, but he whimpered and scurried down the corridor, looking back over his shoulder as if I were the Devil.

To my relief, the tuberoom doors were locked during the sleeping period. But my nerves were taut with expectancy. Garheim was obviously plotting some sort of surprise. I remained wide awake, leaning against the bars, watching.

The corridor lights dimmed. Tape-recorded music played softly from the Navigator's stateroom. I entertained myself by picturing how she and I would have behaved toward each other had we met on Earth. She wouldn't have acted impressed when told I was an agent for the Global Counsel, but she'd have let me take her to dinner. Later she might have introduced me to her family.

Just as my daydream grew interesting, the messboy tiptoed down the corridor.

"Come here," I whispered loudly, motioning him toward me. But he gave me a terrified look. Drawing the Captain's large ring of keys from his shirt, he darted to the tuberoom door.

I shouted, "He's unlocking the door!" As Garheim appeared, I banged on the bars with my water can, shouting, "The mutiny's begun!" I cursed my helplessness.

Stateroom doors opened, throwing rectangles of light across the corridor. The mutineers poured from the tuberoom, a dark wave, knives and crowbars glinting dully. The wave spread out as the Navigator fired into it from her doorway. She and several others ran forward to the control room, the wave at their heels.

One man flopped about on the corridor floor like a stranded fish. Another turned back and speared him with a crowbar. Garheim's hoarse voice shouted for the men to break into the control room, but a volley of shots drove them back.

In the dimness and confusion, I couldn't follow the action or see if the Navigator had escaped. I shouted and raged. I heard someone being killed in his stateroom. The mutineers ran back-and-forth across the corridor, breaking into staterooms, hunting for guns and victims like blood-mad hounds.

They paid no attention to two of their own number on the corridor floor. The cook shouted for mercy, but his words died in a hacking cough. In the cell next to me, Rod and Ed shook their bars and shouted for release. A man ran over, flinching as bullets whined down the corridor. He unlocked their door, and they shoved it open, forcing him to step backwards into my arms.

While other mutineers ran heedlessly by, I jerked that one's head against the bars and strangled him there. The keys dropped from his limp hand. As I unlocked the door, rapid fire from the control room drove the mutineers through doorways, from where two men returned fire with captured pistols. I saw I had no hope of reaching the control room alive; I'd stop bullets from both sides. I edged along the wall toward the stern, then darted into the tuberoom. There I found a seam-scraper—an eight-foot metal rod with a sharp point—and an idea.

Feverishly, I unbolted a section of the floor, exposing the insulated cable that fed the corridor's magnetic gravity circuit. After I located a well-insulated hacksaw, I opened the tuberoom door a crack, and shouted down the corridor,

"Navigator, this is Smithy. I'm for the officers. Hold your fire. I'm going to make a dash for the control room."

Bullets spatted against the door, but I kept shouting.

Finally the Navigator's voice shrilled, "Don't try it, Smithy! The mutineers are waiting for you in the doorways."

"Have the door ready. I'm coming anyway," I shouted as I sawed through the cable. It fed gravity alright! My saw floated one way, and I floated the other. A human dirigible, I push-pulled my way down the corridor with my makeshift spear while hearing dismayed shouts from the mutineers.

As I came abreast of Garheim, I saw him hanging from the wall like a giant ape, swaying back-and-forth as he tried to sight his pistol on me. At a range of no more than twelve feet, he fired. The bullet zipped past my ear, and the recoil jet-propelled Garheim backward into a stateroom. The same thing happened to another gunman. He fired once, missing me by yards, flew back and vanished.

As I neared the doorway to safety, four mutineers floated out at me from the Captain's office. I turned my pole into a spear and jammed the nearest one. But the thrust barely punctured him, sending him head over heels against the control room door and shoving me halfway down the corridor. I swam forward into a nightmare battleground, where we fought upside down, on the walls, along the ceiling. We maneuvered like clumsy blimps, each blow shoving us apart unharmed. Garheim drifted from a doorway.

"Corner him," he yelled. "I'll hold him with one hand and shoot him with the other."

My back against the ceiling, I fended them off with my spear, until a man swam in from behind and grabbed my foot. That was a mistake, giving me a solid target to drive my spear into. But his death agonies were my downfall, for he wouldn't let go of the spear shaft and others caught my legs. Garheim swam up for the kill.

A volley of shots from the control room knocked one of my attackers down the corridor, punched a hole through my thigh, and sent the rest of the mutineers swimming for the doorways. I went for the control room door, unsure whether I was a target or being rescued. The Navigator jerked me inside. I slumped to the floor, since their gravity was still working, and stared into the muzzle of the Captain's pistol.

"It's a trick," he barked, "I'm going to finish him off." But the Navigator clung to his arm.

"I tell you, Smithy's all right," she sobbed.

"I was the guy who warned you!" I shouted.

"Oh Captain, Sir," Hamlet the First Officer said, "I think, if you think, if it's safe we better keep this one— don't you think so sir? There are so few of us left."

For once Hamlet hit the nail on the head. He, the Captain, the Navigator, and I were the only survivors.

"Take charge, Smithy," the Navigator whispered. "I'll try to handle the Captain."

"Guard the door," I told Hamlet.

"Door, SIR," he amended.

"Stow that guff, buddy, get on that door!"

I checked the manhole. It was still locked.

"Captain," I said, and his jaw tightened at the sound of my voice, "how long have you been sending out distress signals?"

"Distress signals? You greenie! You yellow tube-wiper! I've never had a ship in distress. By all the stars in the heavens, my ship goes to Neptune!"

"No distress signals? Listen captain, the mutineers have stopped feeding the tubes. Can't you feel the ship decelerating?"

"I've never lost a ship!" He swayed on his feet, jaw quivering.

"But there may be a space cruiser on Neptune, or closer. There's still a slight chance we could put a boarding party on us before Garheim thinks to cut through the door with oxy torches."

"I've never lost a ship."

"You've lost one now, Captain."

His lower jaw sagged limply. His eyes widened, but I knew he couldn't see me anymore. For Captain Rawn, the brave explorer, had rocketed out into that starlit universe that knows neither beginning nor end, where no ship is ever lost. The tired old body he left behind permitted the Navigator to lead it to a seat. There he stared sightlessly into space.

After helping me bandage my thigh wound, the navigator began beaming radar signals at the grey-domed city on Neptune. From there, they would be rebroadcast to all inhabited planets. The entire solar system would learn that the once-famous explorer, Captain Rawn, had lost his ship, that mutiny had provided a black ending to his long career. All spacemen would gather together, whispering and shaking their gray heads. How the mighty can fall.

Through the nose port, Uranus glowed bigger, brighter than the moon appears from Earth, a deadly blob of green clouds surrounded by its satellites. Were we off course?

Behind me, Hamlet piped, "I think they're pushing a neutron shield at the corridor." Our bullets buried themselves ineffectually in the thick lead. Shortly, the shield must have blocked our doorway, as I heard the hissing roar of an oxy torch. Garheim had figured all his moves.

A red spot the size of a cherry appeared near the top of the door. Soon it was as big as an apple. The whole door began to smoke and glow. Where the cherry had been was now blinding white. Shading my face with my hand, I walked as close as I could bear the heat, then lined up my pistol sights on the white spot.

When the dazzling tongue of the flame burst through, I pulled the trigger. The bullet smacked the nozzle of the torch. The flame vanished. Outside, someone screamed with pain. From confused shouting and cursing that followed, I gathered that the operator had dropped the torch on someone else. It seemed they were having trouble relighting the torch while dealing with the wounded man.

But where was Garheim's voice? He should have been loudly shouting orders. As if answering my question, a deafening clang reverberated through the control room. I whirled and saw the manhole lid swing open, from the padlocked side. Someone had quietly sawed at the hinges from below, and a blow from a sledgehammer had broken away the last strip of metal.

The Navigator screamed. Out of the hole floated a mechanical man with arms and legs of jointed plastic, bulging chest, and a neckless helmet with narrow rectangular view-plate.

"Space suit," Hamlet gasped. Our bullets scattered off its plastic armor causing it to spin like a lazy top, for the non-magnetic suit was unaffected by our gravity floor. Before it could recover, Hamlet, with savage courage I'd not dreamed he possessed, leapt on its back. He hammered with his pistol butt at the tubes connecting the helmet with the oxygen tank.

As I moved to help him, a second spacesuit rose from the hole. This one was deadlier than the first, for the arms of the suit had been sawed off at the wrists. Bare, pale, small hands protruded, one hand holding a gun.

That space-suited mutineer shot the motionless body of the Captain, and the shock of the bullet somehow brought back the mighty explorer from his private universe. With a deep-throated shout he lunged at the monster and attempted to wrestle the gun from its hands.

As the Captain was smashed to the floor, I thrust my gun at one bare hand and fired. The pistol bounced from its bullet-torn fingers. The man in the spacesuit turned to flee, colliding with a third spaceman's helmet and arm rising from the hole.

I grabbed the wounded one from behind, and forced it down upon the emerging one, pushing them down like struggling corks. As the lower one disappeared into the blackness of the ore hold, I saw through its viewplate the narrow red-cornered eyes of Garheim.

As I slammed down the lid, the Navigator cried out, not with fear or pain, but anger, while attacking the remaining space-suited mutineer with a crowbar. Hamlet's thin body lay crumpled on the floor. The suited mutineer swam feebly about the room, pawing at its oxygen tubes.

"Leave him alone," I shouted, "he's suffocating." I beckoned for the suffering mutineer to come to me, but I didn't want to step off the manhole lid. In desperation, he came close and allowed me to unscrew his helmet. The young man inside the space suit begged me not to kill him in cold blood. Hadn't we eaten at the same table?

"Take off the rest of your suit. You have your life, for the moment. But a space cruiser is on the way to our aid," I bluffed. "You can't win. Tell the rest of them if you throw Garheim out the airlock and go back to stoking the tubes, we'll testify that he and those of you who are dead were the ringleaders. The rest of you were little more than innocent bystanders."

He nodded and dropped down the manhole, then I welded the lid shut. I hoped my strategy would at least cause dissension in their ranks.

We had no way of knowing if Neptune had received our distress signals, since the Sky Dagger had wandered far off course. Neptune's radar beam would have to find us before it could answer us.

As the ships thrust-speed declined, we made leeway toward Uranus. The eager gravity of that planet tugged at the nose of the ship, making the gyroscopes whirr and strain to hold it on a steady course. But I knew we were edging sideways, beginning to circle in a contracting orbit like a moth about a flame. Uranus would draw us ever closer, until one last cleaning kiss from gravity sucked us through the glowing cloud banks to destruction.

Hamlet was dead. The Navigator cradled the dying Captain, his head in her lap. She wiped foam from his lips as he mumbled and sputtered deliriously about how proud and happy he was to be on his famous first voyage to Neptune. While gasping orders to his ghostly crew, he went limp.

When the Navigator looked up, I pointed through the noseport at Uranus, a green giant filling the sky. She manipulated the controls and the mechanical brain that figured course corrections, and the ship swung its nose away from the planet. But Uranus seemed to chase us, growing bigger all the time. As I watched it through the periscope, I saw we were already within the orbits of its moons.

Garheim must have recognized our danger, for I saw the needle on the thrust speed indicator slowly rising. He had set the men to stoking the tubes.

He banged on the door. "Open up Smithy. We won't hurt you. You can be head man if you want to throw in with us as pirates."

"That's a good story, "I shouted. "Now tell me another."

A cherry-red spot appeared on the door. They'd repaired that accursed oxy torch. When its flame burst through, I tried shooting the tip again. But the mutineers were too quick for me.

I drew the Navigator behind the gyroscopes. I feared they'd begin shooting through the holes. I held her in my arms, while we talked softly about how wonderful things would have been if we had met on Earth. Not as an officer and a tube man, just a man and a woman, two happy people in love.

Garheim burned four small holes in the door.

Suddenly, roaring, dazzling blooms of flame jetted from all four holes, merging into one great twisting fire, so hot and white it was agony to face it.

Garheim had rigged four nozzles on the oxy torch. He was going to superheat the air to burn out the moisture and oxygen and roast us. Nothing could block that flame. There was nothing for me to shoot at. It hid its entry holes and made the red door droop and cry like melting wax.

"How long have we got?" The Navigator gasped.

"I don't know," I said, "but I'm going to take them with us. Uranus isn't far."

We put the ship in a long dive, straight for the green clouds. As the heat thrust searing fingers into my nostrils, I knew we'd be dead long before the ship crashed.

Perhaps Garheim would even have time to re-enter the fiery control room in a spacesuit and head the Sky Dagger out again. Slowly I drew my pistol. As we tried to say what was most important, I raised it behind her back so she would not be afraid.

The flames died.

Garheim shouted, hoarse with fear. "You fools. We're gonna crash."

I didn't answer. We were prepared for death. Let him think we were already dead.

"Pull up!" he screamed, "Pull up!"

Soon they were all screaming and beating at the red-hot door. I heard them hysterically blaming Garheim, raising their voices in a chorus of anger and terror. Garheim screamed in agony, "No, no, not the torch!" and turned quiet.

I shook the Navigator. "We're alright now." I pulled down the control levers. "Don't you understand?" I shouted. "We're alright. We can live. We've won. Garheim is dead. They'll surrender now."

She pressed her face against my chest, and laughed, a strange gentle laugh trembling with pity and disappointment. It was a window on her thoughts, telling me of wonderful things that could never be, love we'd never know and children we'd never have. But it was not a bitter laugh;

there was wistful humor in it, as she pointed at the periscope viewplate.

I saw what she meant. We were overtaking Uranus, too close. The mutineers had not built up enough exhaust speed to tear us away from the planet. There was nothing we could do.

As we plunged into the green mist, that animal instinct that squeezes out the last drop of survival, never gives up, made my hand pull down the landing initiator switch. But we were falling much too fast.

Commander Ross switched off the tape recorder. He thoughtfully rubbed the back of his head and stared at Paul Dixon, Paul Smith, the man who'd stolen his glory with the first landing on Uranus. Then he smiled wanly and gripped the man's hand.

"Smithy, Sir," he said, "I'm proud to know the real discoverer of Uranus."

Paul Dixon grinned and shook his head. "I just want to continue living here. It's a quiet place, a good place to bring up children."

"You shall be permitted to remain, Sir," the Commander said. "You have the first claim. No one can separate you from your land. This is your island, and your children's island and for your children's children."

As the Commander was on the verge of real oratory, a stray thought deflected him. "I take it the water broke your fall. Any mutineers survive?"

Paul Dixon shook his head.

"Then these are all your children's beds. You must have a small army! When can I meet them, and your wife?"

"If you listen carefully, you can hear them laughing now."

Commander Ross jumped to his feet and peered through the window. A small boat was approaching the island, weighted down by a veritable ship's crew of children rowing their mother home.

The commander chuckled. "You know, sir, when we passed through those radioactive clouds, my men were worried. You know: virility, children, that sort of thing. But I see that a short exposure does no damage."

Paul Dixon roared with laughter. "No. Definitely not. No harm at all," he said. "If anything, the opposite."

The laughter of two new friends flooded out over the quiet, green expanse of the New Earth, Uranus.

HAPPY LANDINGS

AFTERWORD: HIDDEN FACTS ABOUT HAYDEN

by Laurie Winslow Sargent

I n the Foreword, I mentioned a recent move and bringing the musty, dusty manuscripts with me. That move was to the St. Augustine, Florida, area.

Hayden himself was born, raised, and died in Santa Barbara, CA.

Imagine my astonishment when I picked up one manuscript after another bearing a St. Augustine address—only 13 miles from my new home! Hayden, AKA Jack, wrote them when he was about 26 years old. I like imagining him at that age, hunkered over a desk in a rented room in a now-historic home on Bridge Street, a home built in 1894 near the Castillo de San Marcos. That old fort construction had begun in 1672. That makes a mere seventy years ago— the 1960s— sound like peanuts. I can't resist driving by that house periodically on Bridge Street and enjoy reading a letter he wrote his parents about the old fort.

One letter from his father sent from Santa Barbara shows something of Hayden's state of mind at that time. His father urged him to return home, lest Hayden isolate himself too much. You see, an ear deformity at birth made Hayden deaf in one ear. He felt self-conscious about it, and it wasn't always easy to hear people, especially in crowds. Yet during his time of semi-isolation in that Bridge Street house, he produced many amazing stories (all the ones in this book written between 1950 and 1952).

After returning to California, Hayden worked at other jobs in addition to writing. He must have been glad, in the '60s, when long hair became popular. Perhaps with his ears covered he felt more confidence, more social. He did real estate appraisal and was also a sixth-grade teacher at Jefferson Elementary (which closed in 1972).

Based on how playful he was with my own children, I suspect Hayden, to me Jack, was a marvelously creative teacher. And while he wore his hair long until his last breath, despite his "little ear" he was full of self-assurance and smiles, gregarious even, perhaps from his interaction with my children but also his love from Jill. After they married, they enjoyed worldwide travel connected with Mom's South American folk art import business.

Devastatingly, in 1992, only three years after they met, when Jill was only 57 years old, she suffered a massive cerebral hemorrhage. Jack literally saved her life. He was assisting her at an exhibit of her imports when she suddenly felt dizzy. As she went to rest in the car, Jack followed her. Within minutes, seeing signs of stroke, he rushed her to the nearby hospital. His quick actions saved her life, and she incurred less brain injury.

Jill retained her wits, humor, and zest for life, but she unfortunately became wheelchair-bound for life. Her pronunciation of words was hard for many to understand. Jack still adored her: they rocked and she rolled down the wedding aisle after her stroke. But the reality is that for two decades he was her devoted caregiver, leaving less time for writing. Perhaps, in their elder years, too much talk between him and I revolved around logistics of caring for Jill, and him as well, as he aged too.

For many years they still retained their adventurous spirits and traveled internationally. Jack boasted about Jill climbing out of her wheelchair to swim with manta rays and dolphins. He wrote prolifically of their travels to Bali, Malaysia (where Jill's son, my brother Frank, was married), then to Ireland, England, and Norway where I and my own family lived for a while.

I have a funny memory of Jack from that visit. We made an exciting journey through the fjords via trains and ferries, then landed in Bergen. After a day of sightseeing, I walked into their hotel room to find 71-year-old Jack and 61-year-old Jill both wearing Burger King paper crowns. When I laughed, Jack grinned, saying, "Well, she is my queen, you know!"

Few of Hayden's sci-fi readers know what an incurable romantic he was, and how that translated also into poetry writing. He became fascinated with the rhythms of poetry and had several poems published in the book *Stepping Stones: A Collection of Poems by Santa Barbara Poets* (Blue Point Books, 2011.)

I wish now I'd said, "Tell me about everything you've ever written!" He was so supportive of others, perhaps he felt reluctant to shift the spotlight to himself. Now it's his turn for the spotlight!

It was an honor and privilege for me to know Hayden Howard as Jack for 25 years. I hope you've enjoyed diving into his creative author mind as much as I have and learning more about him as a person.

For More News About John Hayden Howard and Laurie Winslow Sargent, Signup For Our Newsletter:

http://wbp.bz/newsletter

Word-of-mouth is critical to an author's long-term success. If you appreciated this book please leave a review on the Amazon sales page:

http://wbp.bz/RW

Howard's timeless science fiction tales will
continue to captivate and ignite your sense
of wonder in REAWAKENED WORLDS:
Volume Two, available now!

www.ingramcontent.com/pod-product-compliance
Lightning Source LLC
Chambersburg PA
CBHW070423310726
48977CB00003B/818